"Are you interested?"

Lauren stood at his hotel-room door in her black satin dress, looking at Brett in a way that nearly brought him to his knees. She smiled with carnal intent and he felt all the blood in his body rush south.

This was the woman who had given him a ride earlier and now, looking at her, Brett could barely think of the word *ride* without X-rated images dancing through his mind.

"When I picked you up," she said in a low, sexy tone, "you told me to surprise you." She reached out, touching the tie that hung haphazardly from his neck. "Surprise."

He didn't know what to say—surprise was certainly one of the things he was feeling. And he was definitely interested.

He stepped back to invite her in. "Are you sure, Lauren?"

When she snaked her arms around his neck and pressed against him, he got the answer he wanted. Because he wanted *her*. Now.

Blaze™

Dear Reader,

It takes a large number of people to make a writer's dream happen, and *Pick Me Up* is no exception. There are those who edit, market, produce, and there are those who supply friendship, critique and emotional support through the process. Many of these people are listed on the acknowledgments page. Special thanks to every single one of them, along with the folks behind the scenes who bring my books to the shelf.

A few people deserve special mention for their role in *Pick Me Up*. Jeannie Watt, Nevada rancher and Harlequin Superromance author, is Brett's creative godmother. Jeannie was generous with her detailed insights into cowboys and ranching. Also Brenda Chin helped me bang out a title that has become one of my favorites. Titling is one of the most difficult parts of writing a book, and we had a fun flurry of phone calls brainstorming *Pick Me Up*. Finally, as always, Birgit Davis-Todd is a constant source of support and inspiration. Birgit always manages to see what a book needs and she helps me see it, too.

However, none of it would matter without one very special person who makes it all worthwhile: the reader. So to all of you, my deepest thanks.

Sincerely,

Samantha Hunter

P.S. Look for my next Harlequin Blaze novel, in December 2007. And check out my Web site, www.samanthahunter.com.

PICK ME UP
Samantha Hunter

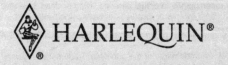

TORONTO • NEW YORK • LONDON
AMSTERDAM • PARIS • SYDNEY • HAMBURG
STOCKHOLM • ATHENS • TOKYO • MILAN • MADRID
PRAGUE • WARSAW • BUDAPEST • AUCKLAND

ISBN-13: 978-0-373-79347-1
ISBN-10: 0-373-79347-2

PICK ME UP

ABOUT THE AUTHOR

Samantha Hunter lives in Syracuse, New York, where she writes full-time for Harlequin Books. When she's not plotting her next book, Sam likes to work in her garden, quilt, cook, read and spend time with her husband and their dogs. *Pick Me Up*, part of the popular FORBIDDEN FANTASIES miniseries, marks her eighth Harlequin Blaze novel to date. Most days you can find Sam chatting on the Blaze boards at eHarlequin.com, or you can check out what's new, enter contests, or drop her a note at her Web site, www.samanthahunter.com.

Books by Samantha Hunter

HARLEQUIN BLAZE

*The HotWires
**Extreme

"Silent gratitude isn't much use to anyone."
—Gertrude Stein

For this book, and for all the books past and future, thank you!

Birgit Davis-Todd, Mike Fratto, Jeannie Watt, Sarah Mayberry, Brenda Chin, Emily Martin, Blake Morrow, Laura Barth, Julie Chivers, Sherie Possessorski, Amy Chen, Peter Cronsberry, Maureen Stead, Page Traynor, Dee Tonorio, Larissa Tchoumak, and Elizabeth Goncalves

1

"ARE YOU SURE you know what you're doing?"

Lauren Baker watched the road before her with no small bit of fear. She was just south of Tucson, and to say the route curling down into the desert canyon was steep was an understatement. Raised in Connecticut, she'd never in her life encountered such death-trap roads as she was discovering in Arizona. It wasn't exactly the time, and definitely not the place, to be distracted by the question her best friend, Becky Saunders, had asked her this morning when they'd spoken on the phone.

Was she sure? Hell, no. That was the whole point.

She was a week and a half into her no schedule, no destination, no obligations trip around the country. She had a map, two credit cards, her cell phone and what clothes and extras fit into the trunk of her Toyota Corolla. Everything else—not that there was a whole heck of a lot—she'd left with Becky for her to sell.

Lauren inched around another excruciatingly sharp curve, ignoring the drop of several hundred feet to her right, fighting the impulse to shut her eyes. Roads like this would challenge any driver, but since acrophobia topped her long list of fears, not freaking out was her main challenge at the moment.

"C'mon Lauren…buck up!" she told herself. "This is all part of your new, no-wimping-out life, remember?"

An only child of parents who'd wanted a large family but didn't end up having one, she'd grown up center stage. 'Overprotected' would be a mild description of her childhood. Not that it had been bad or anything, but it had led her down a certain path and now she was trying to carve a new one for herself.

Her mom and dad didn't shower her with love, they'd drowned her in it. Knowing so much of their happiness revolved around her, she'd grown up not wanting to do anything that would disappoint them.

They'd supported her decision to divorce Wes. However, it hadn't all been smooth sailing. They'd been very upset when she'd refused their offer to come back home after the split. They hadn't understood how she needed to strike out on her own, after escaping Wes's smothering possessiveness.

She'd never had an argument with her parents—not one—because she'd never rebelled. At twenty-nine, it was long past due, though it still made her sad to have hurt them at all. She wanted to be her own woman, but in their eyes, she'd be their little girl forever. Thank God the same could not be said about being Wes's wife.

One of her father's ace employees, Wes had been Lauren's first lover, her husband and her first big mistake. She intended to learn from it.

Wes had her parents' stamp of approval, which she realized now was in part because they had figured marrying Wes would keep her close. Although they'd assumed he'd continue to work for Lauren's father, they'd been very supportive when Wes had decided to break away and start his own business with Lauren. Equal partners, supposedly.

Instead, it had been the beginning of her personal nightmare. Wes had never been physically abusive. He hadn't even been verbally abusive in the technical sense—unless you counted him asking her to account for every minute of her day and his endless questions about her activities, friends and whereabouts. Eventually, explaining everything to him had become impossible, and she'd just stopped going out, which had been a big mistake.

He'd won.

Together they had operated a successful, and profitable, consulting business. Lauren's specialty was as an efficiency expert—she would go into businesses and streamline their production methods and anything else that was causing losses within a company. As a sideline, she'd also started consulting on the home front—helping people with time management and organizing their space.

Wes had put the kibosh on that just as she was building a substantial client list of her own. When she'd received flowers from a man she'd helped, an innocent thank you, Wes had made her life miserable until she had given up her home consulting.

Little by little, he'd stopped scheduling her for outside appointments, hiring a new employee to take over her accounts, relegating her to the home office. In an attempt to save her marriage, she'd gone along. *Stupid, stupid, stupid.*

By the time she'd recognized she had a serious problem, she had no friends, rarely saw her parents and almost never left the house. Deciding to take back some control, she'd called an old friend to go shopping. When Wes arrived home and discovered she wasn't there, he'd flipped out. He forbade her to ever leave the house without his knowledge again. That week she'd moved in with Becky, and the next month served Wes with divorce papers. And so here she was, driving down these winding desert roads.

Tears stung her eyes as she tried to focus on the road. Her parents would be happy once she figured out her life, even if they remained baffled in the meanwhile.

Taking a deep breath, she applied slightly more pressure to the accelerator and worked her way more smoothly around the next curve. Smiling, she let out a whoop of success.

No more letting anyone run her life but her, no more living in fear of what lay around the next corner. No more playing it safe. Playing it safe had only led her down the wrong roads, living her life for everyone except herself. There was so much she had to experience, and now was the time to do it.

According to the map, there was a town called Soul Springs—nice name—at the bottom of this canyon. Maybe she'd stay awhile, who knows? No plans, no limits. That was her motto.

She sang along with the music blaring from her radio, chasing away the crippling ghosts of the past. The clear blue desert sky spread out before her. Dizzying heights aside this was some of the most spectacular scenery she'd ever laid eyes on.

"Whoa!" she yelled, sucking in a breath and hitting the brake, panic overcoming her when a motorcycle zoomed out from behind her, feeling as if it were going to rip off her hubcaps it skimmed so close. The loud rattle of the bike's powerful engine deafened her momentarily, adding to the shock of its sudden appearance. In a flat second, the speeding cyclist was gone, literally leaving her in his dust.

Pulling to the side on a small turnout, she put the car in Park and took several deep breaths, stilling her shaking hands and pounding pulse.

"Jerk!" she spat belatedly along with a number of other choice words at the daredevil who'd almost scared her to death. Who drove these roads like that? It was irresponsible, dangerous and just plain stupid.

"Might as well stretch my legs and let that moron get as far ahead as possible," she muttered. Getting out, she walked over to the passenger side, a safe distance from the edge, trying to enjoy the view.

Frowning at her own apprehension, she took a step forward. There was nothing to be afraid of— the guardrail was there, and it wasn't like someone was going to push her over the side. It was a stunning landscape—she should take a look.

No wimps allowed.

One more step forward, then another.

Adrenaline pushed through her, the crazy motorcyclist forgotten as she stared out over the valleys and mountains, awestruck. The dry wind was hot on her face, but the heat relaxed her, permeating her skin, claiming her.

"Oh my God," she breathed the words out, feeling…overcome. It was just so beautiful. Opening her arms to the vast space, she laughed, and then laughed again at her echo.

"You've come a long way, baby," she joked to herself, feeling cocky and brave. She risked a look down past the rail and stepped back quickly.

"Okay, well, baby steps," she reassured herself,

shuffling back to the solid safety of the car, but still smiling.

Back behind the wheel, she was looking forward to what she'd find at the bottom of the canyon more than ever.

Switching the radio channel as she took the next curve, she looked up, surprised to see that daredevil motorcyclist again. She thought he'd be long gone by now, but no, there he was.

The bike was parked, its slanted posture mimicking the way the man who rode it leaned against the guardrail as if there weren't a sheer drop on the other side. More amazing, he was standing there in a tux, the collar ripped back, his black tie hanging crookedly.

She drove up, got a closer look—square jaw, dusty, sun-bleached sandy hair—she wasn't sure what to make of him. Part *GQ* model, part *Road Warrior*. Maybe she'd give him a piece of her mind for passing her so hazardously, but something about his expression and his posture suggested that maybe she'd be better off driving by. A lifetime of training in good manners wouldn't allow it though; he could be in need of help.

He was tall. The wind had apparently whipped the crap out of what was once a lovely boutonniere. When he fixed intense green eyes on her, she met his stare. There was something wild in that look, a feral gleam.

She rolled down the window. "Is everything okay?"

"Broke down." Nice voice, not as smooth as she would have expected, given the tux. The voice was definitely *Road Warrior*, low and dry.

"Lucky you're alive at all," she said under her breath. He might have heard, but he didn't say anything. She tried again.

"On your way somewhere?"

"Not really."

"Do you have someone coming to get you? Triple A?"

"Nope."

Lauren weighed what to do. He wasn't being very cooperative.

"Do you want a ride?" The words were past her lips before she could reconsider them.

He appeared to consider, too, pausing, and answered her with one short, curt nod. As he reached for the door handle, she wondered what the heck she was doing. He settled into her small front seat, looked at her and smiled ever so slightly, wiping out every coherent thought she'd ever had.

She never picked up hitchhikers—what rational woman did? But he wasn't exactly hitching, was he? In her experience, most hitchhikers weren't hanging around in designer tuxes, either.

"Where to?"

He paused again, staring out the window, and shrugged. "Surprise me."

BRETT WALLACE was sure he was going to lose his freakin' mind if the woman didn't hit the gas—my God, his eighty-year-old grandmother drove faster. He should have known when he saw the Connecticut license plates. At this rate, they'd never make the bottom of the canyon by dark, and then what? There weren't any streetlights up here, and she was a city girl, obviously. She could barely handle the roads in broad daylight. In the dark, she'd just pull over and quit. He snorted to himself. Tourists.

He passed a few moments by studying her profile. Not that he couldn't think of a few things they might do in the dark—after all, nothing holding him back now, was there?

She was pretty, he realized as he took the time to notice. Her short brown hair had a slight curl and curved slightly at the chin, framing a face that would be considered plain by some, but which he found attractive. She had that kind of creamy skin that looked like it might melt if you touched it, and a sprinkle of freckles across her nose that added charm. He'd always liked freckles. Her skin was so light—unprepared for the hot temperatures and harsh sun of the Sonora Desert.

"How about I drive for a bit?"

She spared one second to look over at him before gluing her eyes back on the road. To his astonishment, she barked an unladylike laugh.

"Right—the way you were driving that bike? No

thank you. I'd like to reach the bottom of this road alive."

"If we ever reach it at all," he muttered, blowing out a breath, and admitting only to himself that he *had* been pushing it a bit back on the bike. Maybe more than a little. But by God he'd been pissed and had a perfect right to be, too.

When a guy was racing away from the church where he was supposed to have gotten married just about an hour ago, a little speed was justifiable. He'd had the good luck—and he was counting it as *good*, all things considered—to discover his best man, Howie, in the bride's chambers shortly before the ceremony was to begin. That was unusual, but might not have been a problem except that she'd had her dress up around her waist, and Howie hadn't been helping her with the buttons. With a full congregation waiting, no less.

Howie had done him a favor, he supposed, since he'd been on his way to talk to Marsha, intending to call it off. At least he was going to do her the service of breaking it off, of being honest, though granted, he'd waited until the last minute, as well. Right now he wasn't sure what to think about it, the whole sorry mess.

"My apologies about that. I've been driving these roads for most of my life, and I think I might be able to return a favor and save you a nervous breakdown if you allow me to get us to the bottom before dark."

At the mention of night, her eyes went wide, and after a long pause, she shook her head. "I can handle it."

"Okay then." He sat back, trying to relax, but just getting annoyed. Headstrong women were going to be the death of him.

"Thank you," she answered primly, and he raised his eyebrows. She was wound way too tight.

"Where are you headed?"

"Nowhere in particular," she murmured, and he could tell by the sudden pause that she'd thought better of it a moment too late. Smart girl, she'd just more or less told a stranger she was on the road with no destination, no one expecting her.

"We all need to get away sometimes," he offered by way of convincing her he wasn't a serial killer. He held out his hand. "Brett Wallace. I own a ranching operation back about ten miles. I'm very reputable, depending on who you ask."

He grinned and saw her shoulders ease. "Lauren Baker."

She dared to take one hand off the wheel and gripped his lightly; she had buttery soft hands, her white skin contrasting against his own darker tone. Her touch reverberated somewhere down low in his belly, where he felt a stirring. Shaking it off, he pursued the small talk. It kept him from thinking about how he'd ended up here, anyway.

"Where'd you start from?"

"Hartford, Connecticut."

He whistled. "That's about as East Coast as you can get, huh? They don't have roads like this back there. No wonder you're so tense. You know, it's just a matter of getting into the rhythm of the drive."

"Thanks. I'll keep that in mind," she said sardonically, but he noticed she sped up a little and took the next curve more smoothly.

"So what about you? You live here, you own a ranch. Nice tux," she mentioned meaningfully, asking the question without really asking it.

"Hate these damned monkey suits," he growled, yanking at the collar, even though it was loose. "On my way back from a formal event, and blew something on the bike."

"From the rose on your lapel, I'd guess a wedding. Best man?"

"Apparently not," he muttered in a tone of voice he hoped barred any further questions. Images from the morning flashed in front of his eyes again. How was he supposed to admit that he'd run away from his own wedding, left the bride stranded? Not that she didn't deserve it. Still, it wasn't his way of dealing with things, to cut and run.

Brett couldn't say he gave a damn what people thought most of the time. This time was different. He thought at first it was because he was so angry he might have done something he'd later regret, like busting his longtime friend's skull. But as he'd ripped down the highway on his bike, he'd almost felt free for the first time in months.

Relieved. And guilty. Maybe if he'd stepped up sooner and told Marsha he wasn't sure that they should be getting married, none of this would have happened, but it hadn't seemed so clear at the time. He'd never been in love with Marsha, no more than she'd been in love with him. Their decision to get married was more of an automatic step, the next logical thing to do after they'd been seeing each other on and off for several years. When Marsha had suggested they make it permanent, she'd taken his silence as a "go," and before he'd known it, he was picking tuxes.

It hadn't seemed like a half-bad idea, when he thought about it. He was thirty-five, and the ranch had been his life. He hadn't dated too much since he left college at twenty-two, except for Marsha and a few stray lovers. Marriage had seemed like the thing to do; he and Marsha made as much sense as anything.

But love? No. Neither one of them expected that.

He'd known her since high school, a local girl from a ranch down the line, bigger than his, and more profitable, sure. Marsha liked being involved with things, and Brett had been left with a ranch to run and a thirteen-year-old brother to raise when he was just twenty-three, himself, so having Marsha around had worked out. She knew about ranch life;

they had a decent relationship, good in the sack—or so he'd thought—and she didn't ask too much from him. So he'd let it ride when she wanted to get married.

Until he'd been driving to the church and it hit him he couldn't go through with it—and then he'd found them, and he hadn't known what to think. To pretend to be outraged would have been a lie, but deep down, he was more embarrassed than anything. He'd obviously been less of a man than Marsha needed, as well.

In all the times they'd been together, he'd never seen the raw passion on her face that he'd witnessed her sharing that morning with Howie. That truth stung deep, sticking into a particularly tender area of his male ego that he'd never questioned before. Obviously he hadn't been paying enough attention, in a lot of ways. Romance had never been big on his agenda, but still, a man liked to think he could satisfy a woman, and Marsha clearly hadn't been satisfied. Not by him, anyway.

Maybe when she'd realized he was gone, she'd been relieved, too.

He returned his gaze to Lauren; she didn't seem to mind the lack of conversation. He inhaled the sweet smell of her soap or shampoo, or some damned flowery thing that was attracting him like a bee to a blossom. It was going to be a long ride to Soul Springs, where he assumed his ride was heading. He took another stab at conversation.

"You have any plans once you get where you're going?"

"Not really. Find a place to live, find a job, start fresh."

"Fresh from what?"

"I'd rather not discuss it."

"Fair enough."

She bit her lip and it made him pay more attention to her mouth than he probably should. Turning, he looked out his window. Just because he'd been cuckolded didn't mean he should go jump the first woman he came across.

"I'm divorced," she blurted, and he raised his eyebrows in surprise.

"You don't look old enough to be married, let alone divorced."

"Thanks, but I'm more than old enough to have made my share of mistakes."

"Must've been a bad situation that would drive a woman to the other side of a continent."

"Bad enough."

There was still pain in her voice, and he was curious about why. As he hadn't shared any of his, he didn't feel right asking for hers. Pointing down to the town that looked like a scattering of Monopoly houses from this height, he changed the subject.

"There's Soul Springs. If you can drop me off I can call for a ride and get someone to pick up the bike."

"It's bigger than I thought."

"Part retirement community, part resort. It's a fairly new community, actually, only about thirty years old."

"A senior community? In the desert?"

"Old people love it out here. The dry, hot air is good for what ails them."

"I guess that makes sense. It's beautiful here, too."

"I've lived here my whole life, never tire of it. Can't imagine why anyone would want to be anywhere else."

She pulled down a main street, and he pointed her to a nice-looking motel that he knew was clean and safe by reputation. They got out, and he turned to look at the horizon.

"Might be too late to get help now. I guess I'll wait until tomorrow. Thanks for the ride."

"You're welcome. I hope your bike's okay up there."

"It'll be fine. It's far enough off the road, and if it gets stolen, well, it's insured. I never cared for it much—touchy beast, seems like something breaks every time I take it out." He shrugged, knowing he should be ending this conversation, but was dragging it out. Maybe the more he talked, the less he had to think about what was waiting for him back at the Slanted-W, the name of their family ranch.

She shoved her hands in the pockets of well-worn

jeans that fit very snugly, he noticed when she got out of the car, and smiled as she looked out past the cactus gardens that surrounded the motel.

"Well then, bye. I guess I'll go check in."

As she turned and walked to the door, he couldn't quite ignore the way her nicely shaped backside fit into those jeans, and found himself calling out again.

"Hey, Lauren."

She turned, holding her hand up to shield her eyes from the sun.

"Since we're both stuck here, how about catching dinner? Least I can do to thank you for the ride."

She paused for a moment, considering, and he realized he was holding his breath.

"Thanks, but I'm really tired. I think I'm just going to turn in."

When she turned back to the door, he couldn't deny the bite of her rejection. This just wasn't his day.

2

"IS HE CUTE?"

Lauren grimaced. "Cute doesn't really cover it. Salivatingly hot, or, please-rip-my-clothes-off handsome might be a little closer to the mark. And he's got that whole gruff, young Clint Eastwood thing going for him."

"Wow. God, I love Clint in the old *Rawhide* episodes. I just got them all on DVD, just for him," Becky sighed. "So why'd you turn him down?"

"I don't *know* him. He's just a cowboy or something."

"Lauren, there's no such thing as *just* a cowboy."

"You've known a lot of cowboys I take it?"

"A few."

She could hear the satisfaction in Becky's voice even over the cell phone crackle. Becky was one of the most intelligent women she'd met, but Lauren wasn't sure Becky knew the definition of *monogamous*. Lauren envied Becky's lifestyle, not to mention the confidence and excitement that came with it. Seven years in a bad marriage had left

Lauren severely lacking in that department. It was exactly why she was standing alone in a motel room instead of having dinner with a sexy guy who'd asked her out. Her old, fearful self just wouldn't back down.

"I picked him up on the side of the road, and that's not exactly a safe way to meet someone."

"Is there a safe way to meet anyone? Nothing's ever that cut and dried, I'm afraid. I met one of the creepiest men I've ever known in church."

"You go to church?" Lauren teased.

"It was for my niece's baptism, and don't deflect. Your cowboy doesn't sound like a drifter or a bum, from what you said."

"No," Lauren said, out of excuses. "I didn't get that impression either."

"So what happened to no wimps allowed?"

"There's a difference between wimpy and stupid."

"They sound like the same thing in this case."

"Hey!"

"Hey back. People hook up like this all the time, Lauren. Airplanes, parties, bars. The one-night stand is an American classic, and if done right, with the right guy, it can be something that will make you smile at the memory when you're eighty."

Becky was right. Lauren knew she was right.

That's why she'd called her, to get some much needed courage. Somewhere in this motel, her supersexy cowboy was sitting alone in his room. She wanted to be daring, sexy and spontaneous, but she was wimping out; she'd known Becky wouldn't let her get away with it.

"Lauren, it's one night. An adventure, remember? Go take your cowboy for a ride."

Taking a deep breath, Lauren dug through her large suitcase and pried back the layers of her jeans and T-shirts to retrieve what she was looking for. Finding the package she slowly drew away the tissue, and took in the layers of luxurious black satin.

"I guess this could be as good a time as any to try out the dress," she said with a sigh, holding the shiny fabric in her fingers. The cut of the strapless dress was deceptively simple. She'd bought it on a no-holds-barred shopping trip with Becky the day her divorce had been finalized; it had cost a fortune. She'd never worn it except in the dressing room.

She knew the silky material clung to every curve, not to mention showing off a few she hadn't been aware of. Reaching inside her case, she found a thong, sheer strapless bra and garters with hose. She'd thought it was a waste of space in her sparse luggage, but she couldn't bear to leave them behind.

"That dress was made just for a situation like this. He won't stand a chance."

"I guess I'm afraid of what might happen—what if he thinks I'm a tease, or a downright slut? What if I go down there dressed like this and can't go through with it? What if—"

"Stop what-iffing. Breathe."

"Becky, I was married for so long, I just don't know." Her doubts rang in her mind like a five-alarm fire, and she dropped the dress, watching it collapse into an onyx pool on the bed.

"Lauren, honey, Wes took seven years of your life—don't let him keep getting in your way. You thought you were playing it safe with him, and look what you ended up with. Believe me, you need to do this. You don't have to do anything you don't want to—it's dinner, right? Go to a public place and make sure you have an easy exit route, but do it. And if the best happens, enjoy it. Young Clint Eastwoods aren't easily come by these days. Enjoy yours."

Lauren was so tempted, but was she brave enough?

"Listen, hon, gotta client calling in on the other line, gotta go. Have fun. Don't forget the condoms…"

Condoms? "Becky, I don't have…"

She stopped, pushing the tissue the dress had been wrapped in aside, and discovered a blue rectangular box with a black ribbon wrapped around it. Spiral specialties that studies confirmed intensified sexual pleasure for men and women, so the box claimed.

"Becky, you are a friend among friends," she said to the empty room.

Her decision was made. She started peeling off her jeans, walking to the shower, excitement buzzing every nerve ending. Brett was hot, and she could barely remember what sex was like, it had been so long. That part of her marriage had died a quiet death long before her divorce. And Wes, well, he was handsome, in his stockbroker-like way, but he wasn't a cowboy with dusty, sun-streaked hair and strong, calloused hands.

Stepping out of the shower refreshed a few minutes later, she slipped into the clothes on the bed—the underwear alone made her feel like the sexist woman on earth. The touch of the dress was better than any sex she'd ever had, though maybe it was time to remedy that.

Brett was a question mark, no doubt. It could be the best choice she ever made, or among the worst, but that was what risk was all about, right? She had to do this. Slipping on her low black heels, she took a look in the mirror, applying a scant bit of lipstick, her only makeup.

"You clean up okay, girl." Pushing up her bust and reorganizing a little, she rebelliously made the most of what nature had given her. Grabbing her purse, she made a line for the door.

She'd find Brett's room, and see what happened. Maybe he'd changed his mind, or maybe he'd decided to go back to his ranch. If that was the case, so be it. She'd chalk it up and take herself out for a nice dinner. There, she had a Plan B. No need for nerves. There was nothing to lose.

Opening the door, she paused. Running back to her bed, she ripped open the condom box and grabbed a strip of four or five, shoving them deep in her bag like a guilty secret.

"Never can tell," she whispered before she practically skipped back out the door.

"So what are you gonna do?"

Brett laid back on the bed, contemplating Pete's question and giving his little brother points for not rubbing it in that things with Marsha hadn't worked out.

"For the moment, stay here. I can meet you up there tomorrow, we can trailer the bike back, and see what the heck blew on it."

"I mean about Marsha. She took off you know— Howie, too: She put on a huge act, the bride left at the altar. Made me sick. She took your honeymoon tickets and left. I don't think anyone knows Howie went with her."

"How discreet of them," Brett muttered, rubbing a hand over his face. "I hope they have a great time." On his dime, he thought bitterly.

"You're better off without her, though maybe if you'd listened to me you could have sidestepped some of this trouble. I may be younger, but I know a thing or two."

"Okay, I knew *that* was coming sooner or later," Brett groaned. "You never took to her."

"She's a bitch, Brett, and she's always been one. How you never saw it was beyond me. Howie probably wasn't the first guy she was screwing. Hell, she even came on to me, once."

Brett tensed. "You never mentioned that."

"Why would I? She would have denied it, and you would have believed her. You had your head so deep in the ranch you never looked up to see what else was going on."

Brett shook his head, angry at Pete, but thinking it was probably undeserved, especially since his brother was right. However, Pete also had the luxury of all the things Brett had sacrificed for—Pete had finished his four years at college, and Brett had held down the fort. Pete did his fair share, but Brett held the reins. He took the larger part of managing their legacy.

Pete still held poetic notions of the perfect woman, the perfect relationship. Perfect love. An oxymoron. Brett didn't want to sound cynical or dismissive of his brother's values, but the kid spent way too much time reading poetry by Whitman and Neruda, ignoring the harsh realities of life.

"Anyway, can you meet me out there about noon tomorrow?" Guests at the ranch would be out and about, and the staff would be working, which would give him enough time to come home without drawing undue attention. Still, he couldn't quite shake the feeling that he was sneaking around, and it pissed him off. He had no reason to be ashamed, but he was anyway, and it irked him.

"Yeah."

"I'm going to go find some din—" A knock at the door interrupted his thought. "Listen, I gotta go—see you tomorrow, Pete."

Hanging up the phone, he opened the door tentatively, unaware of anyone who'd be looking for him here, and paused startled when he saw the lovely woman standing before him. He stared for a moment, thinking she had the wrong room. He let his eyes have a little treat as they wandered over her sexy dress—and then he noticed the freckles.

"Lauren?"

She smiled and he felt all the blood in his body rush to his crotch. Shifting a little uncomfortably, he couldn't take his eyes off of her. This was the same jean-clad woman who'd given him a ride earlier?

Looking at her, he could barely think of the word "ride" without X-rated images dancing through his mind. Had he actually considered her merely pretty at any point in time? Had he lost his mind? She was spectacular, sweetness and sin all in one lovely, black satin bundle.

"When I picked you up earlier," she said in a low, sexy tone that was husky, intentional. "You told me to surprise you. So." She turned around slowly, looking at him over her shoulder in a way that nearly brought him to his knees. "Surprise."

He didn't know what to say—surprise was certainly one of the things he was feeling, though no words would seem to form. She reached out, touching the tie that still hung haphazardly from his neck.

"I was just in my room, thinking about you sitting down here in your tux, and I regretted saying no to your offer for dinner. The man at the desk said there are a few really nice restaurants in town, if you're still interested?"

"I'm interested," he managed and stepped back to invite her into the room. Only then he caught her moment of hesitation. While she was coming on bold, the sweet-faced woman from the car was lurking beneath this sexy vixen, and she wasn't entirely comfortable in the role. It only charmed him more.

He stepped back to let her decide, much like he would when he was trying to get a new horse to trust him. No pressure.

It only took her a second to walk across the threshold with determination, as if she'd just made the decision with her entire, beautiful body. He smiled a little as he closed the door.

"Let me just duck in the bathroom, wash my face and get rid of this damned tie, and we'll be off," he said, attempting to reassure her that he wasn't some creep planning on holding her hostage in his room. "I actually do know a very nice restaurant in the resort at the edge of town. Has a glass atrium and low lights so the desert sky shows through."

"It sounds wonderful." She caught his eye shyly, but the color in her cheeks suggested she was as excited as he was.

"That dress is amazing—I didn't even recognize you at first," he added.

"Thank you. I'm glad you like it."

Her voice was driving him crazy. He turned toward the bathroom in case he was tempted to break his promise and did end up taking her hostage. When he came back out she was standing at the window, and he took a moment just to look at her. She had a graceful stance, a natural poise in the way her head was held high, but tilted just to the side. How beautiful those bare shoulders were. She was like something out of a painting, or a magazine, and he'd never known a woman like her, not for many years. Hesitation rose, but he forced it back.

"You're perfect," he heard himself say and immediately felt ridiculous. She turned to him, not saying a word. Her skin was creamy all the way down to that delicious bit of cleavage, and he watched as one sharp, white tooth bit into a bottom lip that shone with a light swipe of color. A black barrette held her hair back in a way he liked and it reminded him of the hairstyles from the sixties that he saw in some of his parents' old pictures. He was itching to release it and thread his fingers through, messing it around her face.

Surprised by his nonsensical urges, he pulled himself together, then noticed she carried only a small purse.

"Did you bring a coat?" He cleared his throat, wondering why he was suddenly so hoarse.

"No. I didn't think I'd need one…"

"The desert gets cold at night, Connecticut," he teased, slipping his own suit coat off.

"Put this over your shoulders on the way to the restaurant. It's not far from here, and you'll be more comfortable." He walked up behind her, sliding the coat over her shoulders, even as she protested.

"No, then you'll be cold. I can just run upstairs and see if I have something to match…"

He left his hands on her shoulders, his face close to her ear. "I won't be cold."

She paused, not saying a word, but the tension strung hot between them, and Brett leaned in just a little closer.

"I like that scent you're wearing—sweet, but not too much so. Fresh, but sort of musky, too, like new rain."

He could see the pulse at the base of her neck picking up a quick, steady beat and her voice wavered when she spoke. "It's a custom scent my parents had made for me years ago. I like it because I can wear it all the time, you know, just every day. It's not overpowering."

He smiled, shaking his head incredulously. "Says who?"

Taking a chance, he nuzzled her neck and grazed his lips over her ear. The tremor that shook her wasn't from fear, unless he was radically misreading the body language between them.

Dinner was becoming less important very quickly. He was hard as a rock, his skin hot, need coursing through him like storm waters rushing over the dry desert floor in a rainstorm. It was quick and unexpected, but he welcomed it. Her response was balm for his masculinity, which had taken a beating today. He squeezed her shoulders slightly, pressed her a little closer so she could feel his arousal and waited for her response. He wouldn't push, but he could hope.

When she lifted her arm and snaked her hand around his neck, he groaned and slid both hands around her waist, just holding her.

"Are you sure, Lauren?"

She looked up into his face, her gaze holding his, but she said nothing, as if struggling for the right words. He didn't have them either, but then again he wasn't big on words. Too many words caused problems, in his view. Touching told him all he needed to know. He ran a thumb over her cheek, examining the freckles that intrigued him so much, trying to reassure her.

"If you say no, it's no—I mean that. Stop means stop. I'll listen, okay? If you want to just leave and go to dinner, that's okay, too," he continued in a low voice, hoping like hell she wouldn't turn toward the door.

He wanted her now, on the spot, but he'd let her set the pace if it killed him, and from the powerful need that was throbbing through him, it just might.

"It is pretty warm in here," she said breathlessly, dropping her purse on the chair, turning and bringing both arms around his neck in such a way as to bring her entire torso in contact with his. Her head fit in underneath his chin as she snuggled against him. Massaging her shoulders, he felt her relax and loosen, all supple heat and subtle curves.

"Lauren," he spoke her name on a whisper, getting used to the sound, slipping his hands up underneath the silk of her hair. Cradling her head, he lowered his lips to hers, tasting gently at first, inhaling the scent that pleased him down to his bones. When her fingers curled into his shoulders and her short nails bit slightly through his shirt, he growled, capturing her breath in a hard, passionate kiss that she met with a fire equaling his.

His tongue stroked hers in a lazy rhythm, and she stroked him back, opening wider, exploring as much as letting herself be explored. He ran his hands over her back, smoothing them over satin down to the curve of her ass and scrunched the material upward until he could reach what was underneath. When his fingertips discovered the thong and garters, he broke away from her mouth, his breath ragged. "Oh, sweet Jesus, Lauren…"

"You like it?"

"You could say that," he joked breathlessly, pressing the hard length of his cock against her hip and watching her eyes widen.

His mouth was on hers again, hungry as he found the dress's zipper and worked it down. Just as he was about to expose all kinds of goodies and take a nice, long look, she put a hand on either one of his arms, stopping him. His progress screeched to a stop, and he froze.

"What's wrong?"

He'd told her he'd listen, and no meant no, and he stood by that. Real men had control—a lesson he lived by, one that was part of his heritage, just as his Dad had always said. Desert ranching was a tough lifestyle, and to be successful at it meant discipline, and Brett prided himself on his. Even so, every nerve ending in his body—some in particular—protested painfully.

She stepped back, out of his grasp, and he nearly moaned with the loss of the contact. How could he want someone so deeply that he'd only met a few hours ago?

She stood about five feet away, holding up the front of her dress with one hand, gazing at him with carnal intent that held him in a trance.

"Lauren?"

She smiled, and he felt relief swell—it wasn't the smile of a woman who was calling it quits. Shrugging delicately, she let the dress fall to the floor and his blood turned thick and hot, his erection begging for release as she walked slowly toward him. The image of her standing there in those sexy undergarments would be with him until he died, he was sure of it.

LAUREN HAD NEVER FELT so wild. So incredibly, absolutely free. Sex with Wes had always been pleasant, ranging from tepid to tame. They hadn't played games or experimented much. In Wes's view, if it worked, why fix it? Of course, it had only usually worked for him.

Standing before Brett in her sexy lingerie, some inner part of herself was emerging after being buried for years, sleeping and waiting to awaken. It felt good— better than good. It wanted to stretch and explore.

As she stepped closer to the bed, she raked her eyes over Brett, taking in the flush of color above his clenched jaw, the way his big hands fisted into the coverlet. She paid particular attention to the impressive bulge in his pants. *She* caused that reaction in him, she realized with delight. Being here with him made her feel like she was capable of anything. Her new, no-wimps-allowed self was sexy and adventurous, and that started right here, right now.

He sat up straighter, reached out and snagged his arm around her lower back, arching her into him and closing his mouth around the tip of her breast, suckling hard through the material of the bra and drawing his tongue over the raspy material that covered the hard nub of her nipple. She gasped and moaned all at once.

"Take it off," she commanded. "I want your mouth on me, and your hands…nothing in between us."

"We have all night, darlin'…plenty of time for all the things I want to do to you…"

"What about what I want to do to you?" she dared to ask and cried out when he bit her lightly.

"There'll be time for that, too," he promised, and his smile broke through any doubts she had left. It was the first time he'd really smiled, and she was enchanted with how it lit up his eyes, softened his gruff demeanor.

Reaching up, he flicked the clasp on the bra open, the band of material fell to the floor between them. He paid close attention to her breasts, massaging and caressing her until she was sure she'd go mad. Her knees were actually shaking. However, patience wasn't her strong suit—it had been a while, and the ache between her thighs insisted that they move faster.

"Brett…I need…I can't take this for too much longer," she managed to tell him on short, labored breaths as bolts of erotic sensations zoomed back and forth from her nipples to her core, burning up every incendiary inch in between.

He finally had mercy, and she nearly sagged backward as he released her. Twisting her by the waist he sat her on the side of the bed. He shucked his clothes in a nanosecond and stood before her proud and aroused. Her gaze drifting over him, she knew she'd made a *very* good decision.

"You're so big." She slapped a hand to her lips, but the words were out of her mouth before she could stop them.

He smiled, taking a step closer, and reached out to touch her hair. "No man minds hearing that, doll."

She laughed, feeling silly and sexy all at once. He was so handsome. Lean and hard, like she knew he would be, with just enough body hair to be manly. She imagined what it would be like to rub her breasts across the wiry hair on his chest, and nearly sighed again knowing all she had to do was ask—or take—and her wish could come true.

Unwilling to wait much longer for what she wanted, she followed her instincts and pushed backward on the bed, propping herself up on one elbow and letting her legs fall apart, the thin strap of the thong her only cover.

She was rewarded by the fierce hunger in his expression, the twitch of that enormous, lovely cock. She smiled, discovering that she enjoyed tempting and teasing, and wanted to see how far she could push her luck.

Easing one hand down between her thighs, she pulled the thong away, showing him everything for just one second until she covered herself with her hand, and flicked just the right spot, eliciting a moan from both of them.

Her head fell back, she was dizzy with pleasure. Who could have known she would be so uninhibited? She certainly hadn't.

She didn't have time to reflect on the issue, though, as the edge of the mattress sank beneath his weight and he slipped his own fingers beneath the thong, replacing hers, settling himself between her legs. Easing her legs farther apart with his wide shoulders, he took the thin strap of the thong in his teeth and snapped it, freeing her, and leaving her completely exposed to his view.

Lord, he took his time looking, and she was on fire from it. Being so intimately inspected was a turn on she never would have expected.

"You're perfect," he repeated his comment from earlier. He ran a finger down the center of her soaked flesh and then shocked her in the best possible way as he slid his fingers deep inside, filling her quickly and unexpectedly, her entire body an ongoing ripple of pleasure.

Hardly giving her time to breathe, he joined in with his mouth, working some magic with his fingers inside and maneuvering into a full-on, intimate kiss that shot straight through her. She arched up, blind with the sensation of it as he drew her clit into his mouth and sucked until rapid-fire orgasms had her bucking against him, flying over her body like sparks. It was fantastic, but still she reached for something more, something deeper.

Twisting from beneath him she flipped over on all fours. He followed her signals, moving on to his back and lying beneath her. She lowered slowly, the delicious anticipation of what she was about to do rifling through her. Everything was the first time, and she was letting go like never before.

Moving experimentally, she enjoyed how her nipples scraped against his skin and groaned in pure erotic bliss. He encouraged her, guiding her with his hands planted on her hips, helping her find his mouth as his fingers returned to fill her.

Setting the rhythm she needed, she rocked over him, his oral ministrations working in concert with her own movements. The resulting climax claimed her within seconds. It was bone deep and pure, shuddering though her entire body as she cried out, riding his tongue and fingers until she collapsed from the wonderful strain of it.

"Brett…oh my God…" she panted, drained and exhausted in the most lovely way.

He brought her against him, snuggling her face in his shoulder. While he rubbed her back, she stretched like a cat, aware of the pressure of his erection against her lower stomach. She was anticipating that, and planned to make his patience and creativity worth the wait.

Pushing upward, she looked down into his eyes as she trapped his erection between her thighs and moved in just such a way that he groaned, twisting beside her. He had wonderful laugh lines carved into his face, she noted—probably from so much time in the sun, and what she hoped was a happy life. He had some stubble, and she rubbed her cheek against it like a kitten seeking a pat.

"You're incredible," he whispered, his eyes dark with pent-up passion, his body tight and hard.

"Brett?"

"Hmm?" As aroused as he was, he seemed pre-occupied with running his hands over her, smoothing them over every inch of her skin. She reached up, tipping his face to hers, looking at him meaningfully.

"The condoms are in my bag."

3

BRETT HAD NEVER REALLY cared for the word *bliss*—it was a prissy word—but he was pretty sure he finally understood the meaning of it. In spades. Lauren made him feel like a teenager again. He was excited to an almost painful degree.

He wanted it to last, unable to remember any time he'd felt like this with a woman, or when he'd felt like this at all. Everything inside of him was busting loose, and he was letting it go. For once, he wasn't going to hold back, or think about anything else. There was only her, and what was happening between them.

As he took out the strip of condoms from her bag, his own heart rate picked up, anticipating how it would feel to be inside of her. He wanted to have her every way he could possibly manage in the next twelve hours, and didn't think the four or five condoms would be enough—if they ran out, he supposed they'd just have to be creative.

He chuckled, shaking his head.

"Something funny?" she asked, lying across his bed like a Victoria's Secret model who wasn't keeping any secrets. He stopped, looking at her. He loved looking at her, to make sure she was real.

"No. You're just tempting me to try to exceed my limits."

"All we can do is our best…"

She smiled, crooked her finger, beckoning him in the way men dreamed about a beautiful woman doing. He was on the bed in a flat second, covering her completely and pressing her down into the mattress. He liked the way she felt beneath him, pliant and soft, warm against his skin. She giggled breathlessly as he weighed the entire length of his body against hers, trapping her wrists on either side of her head, capturing her mouth in a kiss that didn't let either one of them breathe for several long, wet minutes.

When they parted, she said, quite seriously, "Could you put one of those on, please? I don't think I can wait."

He didn't have to be asked twice and lifted up, straddling her hips, letting her watch him cover the length of his shaft and stroking himself a few times as their eyes met. Her mouth was swollen from his kiss, her skin flushed. She slid her teeth over the edge of her lip as she lifted a hand and placed it over his, sliding up and down his length together, until he was getting far too close and needed the real thing.

"Brett?"

"Yeah, sweetheart?"

"Do you mind if we talk?"

"Talk about what?"

"No, I mean, will it bother you if I tell you what I want, you know…in graphic terms?"

His eyebrows flew up as he reached down, brushing a kiss over her flushed cheek.

"You mean you want to talk dirty?"

"If that's something you'd like."

"Hell, yeah," he uttered, leaning down to her ear and giving her a demonstration of what she was asking for, telling her in the coarsest terms he could think of what he wanted to do to her, how hard, for how long, and then what he wanted to do all over again. He felt her breath hitch, and knew it had worked for her.

As he settled down between her thighs, pressing against her but not entering, she returned the sentiment, but she upped the ante. Putting her hands on either side of his face and staring directly into his eyes, she told him in the coarsest language he'd ever heard a woman use what she wanted him to do to her, how hard, for how long, and then what she wanted to do all over again.

It was a mega turn-on and before they could say another word, in one smooth move, he lifted her legs up over each of his shoulders and slid inside of her without hesitation, burying himself to the hilt. She cried out in pleasure, welcoming him, and he had to settle for a moment, stilling as he sank inside of her.

"Sweet Jesus, Lauren, you're so tight…incredibly freakin' hot inside…"

She only moaned in delighted response, her breath coming in hard, short pants that kept rhythm with his thrusts. He pushed deeper, her internal muscles clenching around him. God, if there was a heaven, this was it. His body was tied in a thousand tiny knots. When she started to come, he watched her, each of those knots gloriously releasing as his own climax exploded.

He went deeper, and deeper still, his arms wrapped around her thighs, holding her in place, seeking whatever it was his body needed. His mind disengaged completely as sensation took him over, and he followed it wherever it led him. When his vision finally cleared, he was trembling from head to toe. So was she.

He moved over and dropping to her side, drew her up against him. She was hot, slick and breathing hard. She smelled like flowers and the best sex of his life.

"Are you okay? I kind of lost it there at the end, I hope—"

She put a finger to his lips, and whispered, "It was fabulous. But be quiet now."

She snuggled into him and promptly dozed off. Brett chuckled, and did as she said.

LAUREN WOKE UP FACEDOWN, crosswise on the bed, her feet hanging over one end, her head precariously close to tipping over the corner. Her black dress and underwear were spread around the room, which itself looked like it had been subject to a mini-tornado.

"Man, housekeeping is going to love us," she said, laughing, rolling over and noting several well-used muscles protesting in the best way. Her body had never been so delightfully used and she sat for a moment, gathering her thoughts. She counted one, two, three, four—and oh, yes, there was number five—condom packages, and she smiled again.

What a night. Who knew she could be so wild, or that a man would like it?

She felt like a new person—one who badly needed a hot shower.

"Brett?" Sensing she was alone, as she got up she looked around and saw a slip of paper on the table by the door.

Morning, gorgeous. Went to get some regular clothes, and will meet you for breakfast at the café across the street? Don't hurry. I'll wait. B.

She smiled, putting the note down and then picking it back up again. It was a…momento. Something she'd have to keep besides memories of a night she wanted to remember every day for the rest of her life. It would remind her how crazy she could be, how passionate and free. It was like really being herself for the first time. It would also remind her of what being with a real man could be like, someone who wanted her and didn't hold back.

Humming, she picked up her clothes, dressed and walked back to her room, smiling all the way. She'd get a shower, get dressed and have breakfast with the man she'd remember forever. Then she'd get on with the rest of her life.

SHE FOUND HIM SITTING in the café's outdoor seating area, a newspaper in one hand, a cup of coffee in the other. He looked like he was posing for the cover of a leisure magazine, decked out in new jeans, a red button-down shirt and new cowboy hat along with the same boots he'd been wearing the day before. Apparently boots were standard gear, even with a tux.

He didn't see her yet, as she waited to cross the street. It was a little surreal here, she thought. The narrow streets buzzed with activity, like any town, but the air was hot and dry, and everywhere she looked sand, scrub and mountains surrounded them. It was a little like being at the bottom of a large, rocky bowl.

Back home the leaves would be turning, and people would be getting ready for Halloween. It was getting colder, and Thanksgiving was a month away. Here, it was like midsummer, though there were some cardboard jack-o'-lanterns and black cats hanging in windows around the town.

Walking slowly across the street, she felt her

nerves kick in again, as they'd been doing on and off since she left the room. Last night had been a fantasy come true, a baptism by the best kind of fire into her new life. But what would today bring? She'd almost considered just leaving without saying goodbye—guys did it all the time, right? She wanted to preserve the night just as it was.

As she came closer, her mind's eye snapped another picture she'd never forget—he was impossibly handsome. Just about any guy would look good in a tux—and she knew for sure he looked great out of his—but now he looked...*real*. Earthy, natural and strong, he was part of the land around him. He just looked so right, and so incredibly sexy sitting there.

He glanced up, catching her eye, smiling, and she smiled in return, images of everything they'd done together the night before coming back to her suddenly. As she approached the table, he stood and drew out her chair. She could barely say a clear good morning, she was so nervous. He didn't move back to his own chair, but leaned down, brushing his lips across her ear.

"I hope you got enough sleep," he whispered, nipping her lightly on the nape of her neck, sending jolts of desire through her before he straightened and returned to his own seat.

"I passed out, and I feel wonderful, if a little achy," she answered, grinning as her nerves vanished. His touch was magic. What was it about being with this guy? The minute she was with him or when he touched her, it was like she morphed into this new, confident, sexual person.

Wasn't it supposed to be the other way around? Didn't most people tend to get tongue-tied and awkward when they were actually with the person they desired? Not that she was complaining—it felt wonderful to flirt so easily, to feel so free with herself. "I hope you didn't wait on breakfast for me."

He laughed. "I had a little something, but it wasn't very long ago. I'm used to being up early, eating more at the beginning of the day. Luckily the resort down the street runs a twenty-four hour shop, so I got some clothes, showered while you were still sleeping and came down. I'm only about an hour ahead of you. Hungry?"

She held his stare. "Oh yeah."

"Keep looking at me like that, lady, and we're heading back to the room."

His tone was teasing, but his eyes told her he was serious. She smiled, blushing as she peered down at her menu.

"Everything looks good."

"It is."

She made a decision and closed her menu, sitting back in her chair as a waitress set a pot of coffee on the table and took their order.

"This place, this entire town is so incredible. I

look around at these canyons, and can't imagine who came down here and thought, hey, this would be a good place to put a restaurant."

Brett laughed. "Well, a lot of it has to do with where the water is. There's a supply here, good drainage at the base of the mountains, and people in this part of the country tend to gather where the water is. These spots have hosted all kinds of small ramshackle communities over time, homesteaders, mining, ranching, whatnot. Every now and then one of those communities sticks and becomes something more, like Soul Springs."

"Are there actual springs?" She looked around— the place seemed so barren compared to the lush forests and farms of her home state.

"Underground ones, yes. A few years back one of them caved in, creating a pond of sorts where the kids like to go swimming. It's just over that ridge."

He pointed and she tried to imagine a pond in this environment. Water was the norm back home.

"I wouldn't think there would be enough rain here to support ponds and rivers," she commented.

"It comes, and when it does, it comes fast."

"That sounds dangerous."

"It can be. Anything and anyone in the way of a river rushing down a canyon can be washed away, and it happenes from time to time."

"I've always heard there's a lot of life in the desert, you just have to look for it."

Then their breakfast arrived, steaming, aromatic plates stacked with bacon and pancakes for him, and a Mexican omelet for her.

"This is fantastic," she said. He reached over, putting a few slices of his bacon on her plate. She started to protest, but it smelled wonderful, thicker and juicier than the store-bought stuff she was used to.

"That bacon is local and it's the best you'll have in your life. Don't worry—you worked off enough calories last night to eat an entire pound of the stuff."

She laughed at his humor, loving it. Wes would never have ordered bacon, and would absolutely never have joked about sex over breakfast. They ate in companionable silence. When the food was gone and the coffee pot near empty, Brett sat back. Lauren took a deep breath, soaking it all in. This was perfect, but it had to end. She had to be on her way. How did she say goodbye to a man who'd given her so much, but whom she barely knew?

"Lauren."

"Hmm?" She toyed with the handle of her empty coffee cup, hoping he would take the lead and show her how to back away from their association gracefully. He had to have more experience with this kind of thing than she did, right?

"I was thinking we could spend a little more time together."

She was expecting to be let down softly, not propositioned.

"Really?"

He moved his chair over closer, his hand covering hers. His fingers didn't rest, but played over her knuckles in ways that sent sparks of desire shooting through her. She turned her hand over, palm up, wanting him to touch her there as well. He smiled.

"See that? The sheer chemistry we have—I don't think we should let go of it just yet. I know last night was supposed to be a one-time thing, and I'm okay with that if you want to go on your way, but I was hoping we might make it last a little longer."

"You want me to stay here for a while?" Her mind raced. She wasn't sure that she could process what he was saying exactly, though she had to agree with him that they had intense chemistry. While she'd been ready to walk away—in theory—she was open to hearing his side of the argument.

"No, not here. On my ranch."

"You want me to come home with you?" Her voice rose an octave, and he grinned, shaking his head as she blushed again, looking around to see if anyone heard.

"Sort of. My place is a working ranch. But to keep finances in the black, we also run a tourist business from October to March. It's a luxury operation, you know, come to the desert but enjoy all the comforts of a nice hotel while experiencing real life on a ranch."

"I always thought people had to live in the bunkhouse with the cowboys on dude ranches. Eat grub," she teased.

"I don't think the guys would care much for that. They aren't too thrilled with the tourists sometimes, but it's part of surviving in this economy and has led to some experiences we wouldn't have had otherwise."

"Such as?"

He shrugged. "Well, once we had a bunch of troubled kids from the inner city who thought they were so tough until they were asked to help with branding or foaling. It opened the world for them. Maybe it saved a few of them. I hope so, anyway."

Lauren felt her throat choke up a little bit, touched.

"Last year we had a group of senior women come to spend their eightieth birthdays with us for two weeks. They were tough old broads and they taught us a few things." He laughed, and she laughed with him.

"Sounds like a lot of fun."

"It can be. But it's a lot of work, too, though I love it. Can't imagine life any other way. I'd like to share some of that with you, Connecticut. My treat, you can come as a friend of mine, stay in the main house and take part in as much or as little of the place as you want. Relax, sleep till noon, go swimming, riding, hiking—"

"Swimming?"

"We have one of those spring-fed ponds I was mentioning, and ours doesn't go dry. Hang out as long as you want, and we can enjoy each other a little bit longer. Have some fun, and when you want to go, you can go."

She listened, not sure what to think. He was basically offering her a free vacation in exchange for carrying on their affair. A one-night stand was one thing, but this was a whole new level of casual sex she wasn't sure she was ready for.

"I don't know, Brett."

"You aren't heading anywhere in particular, are you?"

"No. Not in particular."

"Then what's the harm? Aren't we good together?"

She smiled, linking her fingers with his. "We're better than good. But it was just one night—I don't want to push it and lose what would otherwise be a wonderful memory."

"That's not it."

"What do you mean? Of course it is."

"I can see it in your face—you think you're paying for staying at the ranch with sex. I didn't mean it like that. I wouldn't insult you that way."

She cringed at hearing him say it so baldly. "I'm sorry, I know you weren't trying to insult me, but isn't that what it amounts to?"

"Not to my way of thinking. I have friends, business partners, family stay for free at the ranch all the time. It's my place, my home. I'm hoping we can spend more time together, but if you want to come just to spend a few days and leave, that's fine, too."

He trailed a finger up the inside of her arm to the inner curve of her elbow, and she closed her eyes, wondering at the power of such a simple touch.

"Wow," she whispered, feeling overcome and knowing she wanted this more than just about anything, but was she ready? Was it right? Smart?

Brett was a good guy who was asking her to spend some time with him, offering her a no-strings vacation. No strings, amazing sex, as well, if she wanted it. An opportunity to experience this wonderful place, and this wonderful man, for just a little longer.

Her old, timid self was *tsk-tsking* at the very thought of accepting his offer, but the new, bold woman who'd had such fun last night wanted to take that finger that he was stroking up and down her arm and suck it into her mouth, among other things.

Goodbyes were not really what she was thinking about.

"Okay. Thanks," she said in a rush, before she changed her mind. Brett nodded, not saying a word, then leaned forward to cover her mouth in a scorching kiss that easily rivaled the desert heat.

BRETT NAVIGATED THE CANYON roads with ease, glad that Lauren hadn't minded him taking the wheel up to the spot where he was meeting Pete to get his bike. They'd taken so long at breakfast and then getting out of the motel—they'd barely made it out of Lauren's room at all—that he would never have met his brother on time if Lauren had been driving.

He'd handled these roads in every conceivable type of vehicle since he was about fourteen years old. Because of Soul Springs, these curves had guardrails. Wait until they hit the dirt roads on the other side of the mountain, down to the ranch, where some edges were lined only with boulders, and some not guarded at all. He smiled, thinking of Lauren's reaction. She closed her eyes every time they took a turn going over thirty miles an hour.

"There he is," he said, spotting Pete already loading the bike up on the back of a trailer.

His younger brother straightened as they drove up, and seemed mildly surprised to see Brett get out of a strange car. Well, how else did he think he'd get up here? Angel wings?

Lauren got out as well, but hung back by the passenger side of the car, keeping a healthy distance between her and the drop on the other side of the guardrail. Brett gestured to her to join them, and gave her credit that after a second of hesitation, she did. However, she didn't come any closer than the edge of the car, keeping her thigh against the solid edge of the bumper. She was pale, and it struck him how severe her fear of heights was. He walked to her side, putting himself between her and the edge, as Pete wandered over.

"I see you got the bike loaded."

"Yeah. You're late," Pete accused without any rancor, his eyes landing on Lauren and taking her in, maybe for just a second too long for Brett's comfort.

"Yeah, slept late this morning," Brett answered offhand. What was between him and Lauren was their own business, and he sensed she'd feel a whole lot better if people didn't know they were lovers. He would, too.

He knew he wanted to keep his private life private—not that he had anything to hide, after all, he was a free man. His former fiancée was honeymooning in the Caribbean with Howie, and that was pretty much that. Things with Lauren were good, simple, and that's how he wanted to keep it. Separate from the mess that was the rest of his personal life.

"Pete, this is Lauren Baker. We met down in the Springs. I noticed her looking at a brochure of ours in the lobby of the Springs Motel, and so invited her for a stay."

It was a harmless white lie, and he saw the relief on Lauren's face. Pete smiled, holding his hand out, and Brett held his breath that his brother wouldn't make any comments about the wedding.

"Nice to meet you, Lauren. Glad my brother convinced you to give the ranch a try."

"Thanks. It sounds like it will be…different."

"From your accent I'd say you come from New England, am I right?

"Connecticut—how could you tell?"

"I went to college out there. Beautiful state."

"Thanks. I'm enjoying Arizona as well."

Brett remained silent through the exchange, though perked up a bit on her response—was that slight bit of huskiness in her tone for him, or was she flirting with Pete?

Surprised to find himself on the hair-trigger end of jealousy, he looked at Lauren and his brother, finding nothing but polite interactions between them. He was obviously going nuts—being jilted had affected him more deeply than he'd thought. Pete finally shook him out of it.

"So, we getting moving, or are we standing here all day?"

"Let's go. I'll drive with Lauren, if we want to get home anytime today."

Pete looked at them curiously, and Lauren filled in the blanks.

"I'm afraid of heights. Makes it hard to drive these roads."

"You get used to them. I'll see you back at the ranch—you go ahead, I'll be slower with the trailer."

"Will do."

Lauren walked back to the car, sliding into the driver's seat, and Brett hung back for a moment, following Pete to his side of the truck.

"Listen, bud, do me a favor."

"Another one?"

"I don't want Lauren knowing what happened yesterday."

Manly understanding crossed Pete's face within moments, and Brett wasn't sure if he'd cooperate or not.

"I see. It's like that, is it? She's your payback? She seems too nice."

Brett clenched his jaw. "It's *not* like that. I just like her, is all. She seems nice, so I invited her back, and it's…uncomplicated. I want to keep it that way. She'll probably take off in a few days or a week, and there's no need to drag her into all of this."

"So how you going to keep anyone else from telling her?"

"Well, no one would have any reason to, would they? She's just another guest at the ranch, and a stranger. Let's just make sure it's not a problem."

Pete shook his head, but agreeing anyway. "It's your call, Brett."

"That's right, it is. I owe you one."

"Heh. One. If you think you're getting off that easy, forget it."

Brett laughed, and walked back to the car where Lauren was waiting, and felt better than he had in days.

4

PARKING IN FRONT of the main house, Lauren watched as Brett got out of the car then opened her door. She took in the stunning, huge stone and adobe hacienda sprawling out before her. She'd never seen anything like it.

"It's gorgeous. I was expecting a big pine lodge or something to that effect."

"You're in the desert, remember," he answered, smiling as he settled his hands on his hips and gazed at his home with obvious pride. "It was built in the thirties. My parents bought it in the sixties and did a lot of updates, but they kept the southwestern style, even with the additions and some of the outbuildings. Helps a lot with utilities, naturally warm and cool."

"It blends into the landscape so beautifully," she commented, the efficiency expert in her loving the simple charm of a building and that it had environmental benefits was a bonus.

"Back when it was built, there weren't as many outbuildings. Those were added through the years. Most of the staff live in their own homes, though the cowboys stay in the bunkhouse, just like in the old days. There are always changes going on, but it's really just home to us."

"Isn't it strange to have guests here so often?" Lauren knew many of her friends, especially those on the Cape, often rented out rooms during the summer vacation season, but she'd never been able to imagine sharing her home with strangers.

"Sometimes, but it's only for a few months out of the year, and aside from keeping us in the black, most of the people who visit become a little like family while they're here."

"Are you sure you can spare a room in your house? I'd gladly stay in one of your other accommodations."

He stepped in a little closer, leaning down to whisper in her ear, "I want you close. I'm right down the hall."

She smiled faintly, heat erupting between them, but she couldn't deny her reservations now that she was here. Was she doing the right thing? There was chemistry between them, still she promised herself not to stay too long. Brett didn't seem to notice her hesitation and led the way.

"C'mon, let's get you settled. We'll go in, meet everyone and I'll send someone out to get your stuff. They'll park your car down by the lower stables. If you need it, you could take a hike down there through the pasture, or someone can give you a lift down there anytime."

"Okay." She dusted her sweaty palms against her jeans, and followed him into the house, which was just as stunning, if not more so, than the outside. It was cooler inside, just right, in spite of the fact that there was no hum of air-conditioning anywhere, just the quiet whirling of broad-bladed ceiling fans.

Exotic, potted cacti, some as tall as she was, bloomed in most windows, and many were flowering. The furniture was large and solid, the upholstery in colorful, warm southwestern prints. Paintings and sculptures were scattered around the room. The walls were lined with bookcases crammed full.

There were plenty of places to sit, some circling the fireplace on the far end, and the rest around a supersized plasma television on the other wall. It really did look like a home, not a hotel, and Lauren became more comfortable immediately.

"You okay?"

She smiled. "Just looking around. You have good taste—love the furniture and how you've managed to create a space for different activities, and yet make it all very communal. And there are no stuffed animal heads on the walls," she teased.

He laughed. "I don't know much about it, to be honest. My mother wouldn't have animal hides or horns on the wall, she was too much of an animal lover. Sherry and Mar— uh, Sherry takes care of that kind of thing, for the most part."

"No hunting trophies, then?"

"We actually don't hunt too often, unless we have a predator coming after our stock. The wild pigs can sometimes be a problem."

Before she could respond, they were interrupted by another person entering the room.

"Hey, Brett—didn't expect to see you here today."

Lauren looked at Brett curiously—why wouldn't they expect to see him? But Brett wasn't looking at her, he'd turned to meet the other man, grabbing his hand in a quick shake, his back to Lauren.

"Yeah, hey Deke. Got stuck over in Soul Springs, but made it back just fine. Pete's bringing in the bike. How're things going around here?"

The tall, older man took a long assessing look at Brett and then turned his attention to her. Lauren felt a little disturbed by how closely he checked her over. She took his rough hand in a handshake when he offered it, but drew hers away when he held on just a moment too long.

"Things are things. Who have you got here?"

"This is Lauren Baker. She'll be a guest at the ranch for a while."

Deke smiled. "Always room for another pretty lady around here."

Lauren smiled; his comment was perfectly polite, but there was something of a leer in his gaze, and the hairs on the back of her neck stood.

"I met Lauren over in Soul Springs. It's her first

time out west, and I invited her to experience real western life for a little while."

"I'll probably just stick around for a few days and be on my way," she clarified.

"You're welcome for as long as you like," Brett added, and then turned his attention to Deke.

"You taking a group out riding today, Deke?"

"Yep—just heading down now."

Brett nodded. "I'll let you get to it then."

Deke didn't say anything, sliding her another odd look, and nodding back.

"Nice to meet you, miss." He tipped his hat, winking at her. "I hope you have a good time."

She murmured a thank you, yet felt relieved when Deke left. Brett took her into the kitchen—which was the size of her entire apartment when she'd been in college—and introduced her to some more people.

There was Sherry, who smiled only with her lips when Lauren was introduced. Lauren placed her in her late forties, and married, if the rings were any indication. Sherry was a knockout, Native American beauty who ran the bookings and hospitality business even though she didn't come across as particularly hospitable.

In fact, Lauren felt slightly intimidated, which she almost never did with other women. Still, there was just something about how Sherry was looking at her, as if she were accusing her of something. *But what?* She couldn't have designs of her own on her boss, could she?

Then there was Davie Suarez, the cook, who was busy planning that evening's dinner and didn't say much. He spoke so softly she almost couldn't hear him when he told her to enjoy her stay. He had gentle brown eyes and handsome features that Lauren knew probably made the girls turn inside out.

"Are you sure it's okay that I'm here?" she asked Brett as they walked down the hall and up some stairs to what Brett referred to as the "private" section of the house.

"It's my home, Lauren. I own it, I run it, and I can have anyone here that I damned well please."

He must have realized how agitated he sounded, because he stopped and faced her, running a hand over his face, blowing out a breath as they paused in front of a door.

"Listen, everything is fine. I probably should have called ahead to let them know I was bringing someone home, but having another guest at the table is no big deal. Davie always makes more than everyone can eat, and Sherry just takes her job very seriously. She probably just didn't like being surprised because she couldn't get a room ready for you, with all the usual amenities she arranges for all guests."

"All paying guests," Lauren corrected.

"But you're *my* guest. It's personal, and it's not the first time I've had friends stay here, so please, don't worry about it. Here's your room," he said, opening the door. She stopped, snagging on to the subtlety of the comment he'd made.

"You say you've had *friends* here often…?" She wasn't sure she was comfortable being a notch on the bedpost, especially if there were a long line of notches. A one-night stand was one thing—they existed out of time, out of context—but this was something else altogether. Were people sliding her strange looks because she was yet another in Brett's long list of conquests? Considering how hot he was, it wouldn't be a stretch.

He grinned rakishly, understanding what she was asking. "I don't mean those kinds of friends, though there may have been one or two. Take it at face value, Lauren. I'm not a complicated guy."

She relaxed letting the issue go as she walked in past him and inhaled the spicy male scent of his soap, forgetting about her worries as she scanned the room with delight.

"It's charming! Are all of your rooms this cozy?"

There was a queen-sized bed covered with a hand-made quilt, thick pillows and, next to it, a colorful throw rug. An oversized wing chair sat by the window, ideal for reading or just staring out at the mountains with a desk adjacent to it. The décor had a particularly female touch.

"This is part of our family quarters, so it's really more homey than the guest rooms. We've tried to make them all comfortable and welcoming, but they're more—"

"Standardized."

"Yeah, that's as good a word as any. This actually used to be my parents' office, but we converted it into a guest room after they were gone. My mother picked out that rug on their honeymoon."

Lauren knelt close down to the rug, inspecting it closely. "It's an extremely high-grade wool—see how close these knots are? I think it's Kurdish, but I'm not an expert. It's gorgeous, though, and probably worth a fortune."

Brett lowered down next to her, running his hand over the carpet, a fond look on his face.

"My mother loved rugs. I don't know the history of this one, but she thought things were meant to be used."

"That's so different than how I grew up." She sighed, thinking of all the beautiful things her parents collected that no one was allowed to touch. Lauren smiled—she'd been one of them, in a way. "Your mother had excellent taste, and I like that philosophy of using things," she added quickly, not wanting to seem too materialistic.

"Thanks." He looked at her sidelong with a smile that chased her doubts away. Swiveling to a sitting position, he drew her into his arms and kicked the door shut in one smooth move. "Come here. It's been too long since last night."

His lips fastened over hers, the unexpected kiss taking her breath away, but who needed oxygen when she had Brett instead? She wiggled into a more comfortable position on top of him, bracing her hands on either side of his head, returning the deep kiss with everything she had.

"No more doubts," he whispered against her lips when he released her.

Smiling, she just nodded, not really feeling the need for words and lowered her mouth to his to avoid them.

SOMETIME LATER, Brett closed the door, his body hot and his blood hotter. They hadn't ended up doing the deed, but only because there wasn't a condom in the room. He wouldn't be so forgetful next time.

He smiled as he walked down the hall, thinking about how he hadn't made out with a woman for probably more than a decade. He and Lauren had kissed each other's lips bruised, touched each other everywhere until they could hardly breathe; the passion had been thick and senseless, but nary one piece of clothing had been removed.

It had been tremendous fun and he'd loved every single second of it. He couldn't remember a time when he was an adult that a little kissing hadn't led to a foregone conclusion, but he found a little anticipation only made thinking about the eventual result all the sweeter.

However, passion wasn't the only thing warming him. He didn't talk about his parents much, even with Pete. However, with Lauren, it seemed natural. Everything was easy between them, and he hadn't really ever experienced that with a woman. Things had been easy with Marsha because he'd just gone about ranch business and let her have her way on things, where they went, what they did, but with Lauren, it was more of a mutual thing. He liked it.

Lauren was the kind of person who paid attention to details, to little things that were nonetheless very meaningful. Not everyone had that quality, certainly Marsha hadn't—she would have wanted to move that old carpet into storage. He'd never really thought about it at the time, but hearing Lauren's admiration of his mother's things had moved him.

"You look awfully happy for a jilted groom," Sherry said casually as he returned to the kitchen, but there wasn't anything light about the look she shot him.

It was no wonder why. Sherry and Marsha were friends, and it was going to be a difficult dance to keep business and personal things separate. Sherry was the best person he'd ever had running the reservations and hospitality end of the business, and he knew she put out a lot of fires that weren't necessarily her responsibility, either.

She was honest, opinionated and a good person. However, that didn't give her permission to judge his personal choices, or his situation. The boundaries between friendship and work sometimes blurred, but this time he wanted them to be perfectly clear.

"I'm good, Sherry. Thanks for asking. But I'd rather not make what happened at the wedding the subject of kitchen chitchat, if you don't mind."

Good thing about a straightforward person like Sherry was that you could be straightforward right back.

"Marsha was heartbroken, Brett. It just doesn't seem your style to walk out on a woman. I'm thinking there must be more to the story, but she's gone, and you're not saying much."

He wasn't sure how to break the news to his hostess that her friend had apparently played her along with everyone else. "It's just how things work out sometimes," he responded in a tone that should have marked the end of the conversation, but didn't.

"We were all waiting, clueless. And now you bring home another woman? Someone you just met? Poor Marsha—"

It was the last two words that nearly had him turning on Sherry, but he held back. What had happened wasn't anyone's business, and he didn't owe anyone any explanations. If she was going to find out, let Marsha tell her. If people thought the worst of him, well, there wasn't much he could do about it.

"Sherry, you're the best manager I've ever had, and I'd like to think you're a friend. But my love life, and what I do in my home, or who I share it with, is my call. I don't defend my choices to anyone." It was as much as he was going to say, and he said it with conviction.

Some of the color that was high in her cheeks faded, and she lowered her eyes, obviously still pissed, but backing off.

Great. Did everyone really believe he'd just dumped Marsha and ran? How could he set the record straight without encouraging even more gossip—including, no doubt, speculations that he hadn't been able to keep his woman happy. That prospect was just as irritating as people thinking he was a jerk.

He'd probably made a mistake just leaving the church rather than staying and calling Marsha out on her actions, but he hated public scenes.

Even his parents' funeral had been extra painful for him because he couldn't just grieve in private. He'd been stunned to lose both of his parents in a car accident, becoming Pete's guardian and the ranch owner all at once, and everyone was watching him while he did it. But he'd sucked it all in and dealt with business, letting Pete deal with the social side of things—he was better at it anyway.

The gossip would die down if he didn't feed into it. Marsha had screwed him pretty good, but it would pass. People would lose interest, eventually.

Sherry huffed, picking up a stack of papers on

the counter. "Fine. I have to check the activities roster for tomorrow."

"Okay." He started to go, but paused. "And Sherry, remember, Lauren Baker is my guest, and I expect that she'll be treated like one." He made sure he had her full attention when he added, "I expect people will respect our privacy, and not make our problems the source of gossip around here, especially with the guests."

"You got it, *boss*," she said dryly, but he could hear the disapproval in her voice.

LAUREN SAT IN THE CHAIR looking out the window. Young parents held the hands of their enthusiastic children who were nearly dragging mom and dad toward the barns, obviously anxious for the next exciting activity. She saw a cowboy take the little girl who was maybe all of six years old and lift her up onto a horse who stood patiently, undisturbed by the child's squeals of glee.

Lauren sighed, wondering if her parents had taken her on vacations like this if she would have grown up being more daring, more adventurous. They took plenty of family trips, but it was always to resorts or cities.

With no small amount of envy, Lauren continued to watch as the cowboy led the horse slowly around, instructing the little girl. Most of the entertainment she'd been allowed was safe, boring even, compared to sitting up on a very large horse and learning to ride. Her mother had never even allowed her to go on a carousel by herself, afraid she'd fall off. She loved her parents, and they loved her—but was love always so smothering?

Being with Brett was anything but—he set her free. However she knew that was lust, not love.

Her gaze drifted around the room, resting for a moment on the carpet where she and Brett had lay kissing for several long, hot minutes when she'd arrived. Then she studied the bookcases, where books were jammed in every which way, the collection of knickknacks and pieces of western memorabilia scattered around the room. It all contrasted, in a winning way, with the priceless antique carpet and the Tiffany lamp by the bed—real, that she could tell, not a replica. It was a decorative blend of art and kitsch that she never would have dreamed of in her too-orderly world. Cluttered and crazy, maybe even a little dusty and completely homey.

"So why am I sitting here, watching life go by, instead of out there, taking part?" she asked herself, shaking her head ruefully. Old habits were hard to break.

She left the room with a sense of purpose, determined to learn the lay of the land around the ranch, maybe even meet a few people or visit one of the barns. Who knew what could happen? She was open to anything. Ready for adventure.

An enticing aroma led her to the kitchen, where Davie was working among several huge, steaming pots on a large stove. The way he moved reminded her of an orchestra conductor. Suddenly aware of her gurgling stomach, she wondered what he was cooking, and if she could help.

"Hi. Is that lunch that smells so amazing?"

He turned, smiling. He was in his element, and shook his head. "*Enchilada Suiza* for dinner. Normally the guests have cold lunches packed for day trips or they go to some of the local towns touring, but we have supplies here, as well. I could make you a sandwich or a salad," he offered graciously.

"I don't want to trouble you. If you can tell me where to find the ingredients, I'll try to stay out of your way, and make my own."

"It's no trouble. It's my job, and my pleasure," he said as he turned down the heat on a pot while he rummaged through a huge stainless steel, double-sided refrigerator-freezer. "BLT okay? That's what I was thinking of making for the staff lunch."

"Sounds great. Are you sure I can't help?"

He arranged the items on the counter, then placed a slab of thick bacon on the grill. "You are a guest. You shouldn't help in the kitchen."

He sliced several plump red tomatoes and then diced avocados to make a spicy avocado mayonnaise that had her mouth watering. This wasn't going to be just any run-of-the-mill BLT. Davie clearly had a knack for making even a simple lunch extraordinary.

"Brett said guests often took part in all ranch activities, including work."

Davie grinned. "He's right, but none have asked to help cook dinner yet—you're the first."

She smiled back, liking the easy way he conversed while he worked, and she relaxed a little more.

"I like to cook, though I think my idea of cooking may be radically different from yours. That sandwich looks like it's going to be a work of art."

His broad, tanned features shone with pride at the compliment, and Lauren knew she liked him already. After the rather weird reception from Deke and Sherry, it was nice to find a staff person she could feel comfortable with.

She took a chance, hoping he wouldn't think her too pushy. "If you don't mind, I'd love to help you in the kitchen a few times. That would be fun."

"Sure. We'll work something out." He slid the sandwich across the counter toward her, and continued to make sandwich plates, presumably for the other house staff.

"Thanks. I'm not one much for horses and stuff, anyway."

"Kind of a strange place to vacation, if that's the case." There was no innuendo in his voice, no suggestion of anything other than general conversation, and she nodded.

"I never would have considered it, frankly, but I met Brett and he told me about the ranch, and I guess he decided my Connecticut world view needed a little broadening."

She bit into her sandwich and groaned with appreciation—it wasn't a BLT, it was far too exotic with the rich, aromatic avocado spread and the thick, salty bacon.

"This may be the best sandwich I have ever had in my life. It's better than sex," she exclaimed and then slapped a hand over her mouth as she realized what she'd said, but Davie only laughed.

"Thanks, but I think you're overrating the bacon."

She grinned, thinking about her night with Brett, and admitting—to herself this time—that the sandwich wasn't better than being with Brett. As a few people showed up in the doorway, drawn by the wonderful food as well, she wondered if she should leave. Davie took it upon himself to do introductions.

"Lauren, this is Gina, the housekeeping coordinator, and Buck, our all-around handyman, mechanic. If you need something fixed, Buck's the man to do it."

Lauren shook hands with them though they didn't say much. She got that weird vibe again, as if they were thinking things about her that they weren't saying. Was it because she was so new to this part of the country, and she stood out like a sore thumb?

But didn't they have guests from all over stay here? She wouldn't think she was all that unusual.

"And you know Sherry already," Davie continued as Sherry walked in, and now Lauren knew she wasn't imagining things—if the woman's gaze was any colder, her eyeballs would fall out and shatter on the floor like chips of ice. Lauren nodded in acknowledgement and felt her cheeks warm when the woman turned away from her, a blatant snub.

Apparently Lauren was the only one who noticed the slight as Davie sat on a stool at the counter in front of his own sandwich. Lauren felt very out of place all of a sudden, sitting among this small group who probably knew each other very well. She consumed the second half of her sandwich much more quickly and didn't savor the taste as much.

"Sherry, do you know of any other guests who might be interested in a southwestern cooking night?" Davie asked.

"Probably—we haven't done that in a while. Why do you ask?"

"Lauren is interested in taking part in kitchen work, and I thought there might be others, as well. I could incorporate a few nights a week with guests involved, if they were interested. Though Lauren is welcome either way," he said, smiling warmly. Lauren was appreciative amid the daggers that Sherry was shooting in her direction.

What was this woman's problem? Whatever it

was, Lauren wasn't about to buckle underneath it. She lifted her head, smiled gratefully at Davie and made eye contact with everyone around the table, Sherry included. Lauren reminded herself that she was here as a legitimate guest, and she had nothing to be ashamed of.

"Thanks, Davie. I'd like that. I could help out tomorrow, if you want."

"Tomorrow is fine. Just come around whenever is convenient for you, and I'll put you to work."

"Thanks."

She thought she heard Sherry mutter something under her breath, and stared at the woman directly.

"I'm sorry—did you say something?"

Sherry appeared startled, as if not expecting that Lauren would confront her directly.

"There are a lot of things to do on the ranch. Most people don't choose kitchen work. They can do that at home."

Lauren frowned, taking offense for Davie, if nothing else, though he talked with Gina and didn't seem to be listening to Sherry.

"I'd like to learn some of the recipes. I never had much chance to cook when I was home, but I enjoy it. I would imagine many guests would."

"So now you're going to pass your opinion on the activities roster, as well?"

Sherry evidently was more than willing to confront, and Lauren wasn't sure what to say in response to the verbal baiting, but Davie solved the problem with a firm hand.

"Sherry," he said, gently scolding. "Lauren is a guest. She has carte blanche to do whatever ranch activities she enjoys, or none at all. You know what Brett always says—there's no right or wrong here, just fun. Hospitality comes first." He smiled, but his gaze cautioned the hostess, who looked away.

"Of course, Davie is right. I'm sorry if I was short with you. It's been a busy morning. Enjoy your time at the ranch," she said to Lauren as pleasantly as possible, though her tight features belied her words. Lauren, however, decided the further she stayed away from staff affairs, the better.

"Thank you. I guess I'll go out for a walk." She smiled at Davie warmly. "Thanks for the best lunch I've had in ages."

As she went out into the arid afternoon heat, she stood on the porch for a moment, and exhaled deeply, shaking off the tension from her encounter with Sherry. This was supposed to be a fun time for her, and she wasn't going to let a few pissy people ruin her experience.

With that end in mind, she headed toward the barn where she'd seen the little girl on the horse, curious what adventures she might find in front of her for the rest of the afternoon.

5

LAUREN STROLLED ABOUT the ranch for a while, staying close by the buildings, heeding warnings about staying clear of rattlesnakes and other wildlife. She'd never seen a snake up close except in the zoo, and she'd like to keep it that way.

She strode over to the opening leading into the stables that Brett had pointed out on their way up the road, and jumped back when a large horse popped its head over the top of the stall to check her out. She moved to the center of the space between the stalls, smiling tentatively at the large animal.

"You startled me."

The horse stared back with docile brown eyes. She almost worked up the nerve to step closer and pet its velvety nose, but when the animal lifted its head, and snorted, she thought better of it.

Still, she walked through the barn slowly, admiring the horses.

She turned the corner past the horse stalls, expecting to find some guests or a ranch hand whom she could ask several questions. Instead she found Brett's brother Pete in a hot embrace with a woman he had pushed up against the wall, her hands trapped on either side of her head. From the passionate way the girl moaned and arched forward, Lauren assumed this was not unwanted attention.

She tried not to give herself away, but stepped back on a creaky board and the two broke immediately apart. They were both breathing heavily, their faces flushed with desire, their eyes refocusing on her. She backed away.

"I'm *so* sorry…I was just looking at the horses and—"

To her astonishment, Pete just laughed softly, stepping toward her. "Didn't realize you'd bump into two people making out in the barn? That makes sense." His tone was good-natured, so she smiled in acknowledgement, more embarrassed than they were, she figured.

"Still, um…" What did one say in this kind of situation? Maybe the less the better. "Listen, I'll get out now— you two…anyway, have a nice day."

"Hold on!" Pete nearly shouted as she turned, and when she looked back, she found he did appear a bit frazzled. The young woman he was with looked downright nervous, as well. Lauren was picking up strange vibes all over this place.

Pete wiped a hand over his face, softening his voice. "Listen, you're a guest and you came down to look at the horses, so why don't you let me show you around? Graciela has to get back to work anyway."

Lauren's heart melted at the look he shared with Graciela—the two were obviously deeply in love. Would she ever know that kind of devotion again? Or maybe she'd never known it, not really. Wes had been loyal, as far as she knew. Obsessed, controlling, yes, but not devoted in the way that she saw in Pete's eyes.

What would it feel like to have a man look at her like that, with all that emotion pouring forth as if he felt so much that he couldn't contain it all?

As Graciela left, Lauren faced Pete. "I'm really so sorry. I didn't mean to intrude on a private moment."

He smiled, and she was struck by how much he looked like Brett when he did.

"No problem, really. I just get anywhere near her and I can't seem to keep my hands to myself," he admitted, grinning and blushing as he walked back around the end of the stalls, picking up some ropes from the floor. "I'm crazy about her."

"She's absolutely gorgeous, and from the look in her eyes, the feelings are mutual." Lauren found his openness about his emotions sweet and unusual.

"Thanks. I hope so."

"Does she work here?"

He nodded, kicking his toe into a loose board and avoiding her eyes.

"Yeah, she's in housekeeping, though she helps out a little with the horses in her free time, as well.

Most everyone does, since everyone here rides. She always wanted to ride as a kid, but she never got the chance in Mexico where her family still lives. They're very poor, and haven't been able to afford to move to the States."

"It's hard to be alone," Lauren commented diplomatically.

He nodded, his face noncommittal, but Lauren detected strain behind his silence, as if he didn't know what to do.

"Is everything okay?" Lauren gauged how far she should pry into someone else's business, but they'd both seemed upset about something and apparently it wasn't just about her catching them in a clinch.

"It's fine, I mean, I need you not to mention that you caught us like that, you know, together."

Lauren smiled. "I don't know anyone—who would I tell?"

Pete's face was tense with worry as he met her gaze. "You know Brett."

Lauren hesitated. "Your brother doesn't know you have a relationship with Graciela? Why would that bother him?"

"He doesn't approve of us messing around with people who work here. So I'd appreciate it if you would pretend you hadn't seen anything."

Lauren frowned. She wouldn't have exactly been running around stirring up gossip, but she could see how she might have made a passing comment to

Brett. Now she felt as if she was keeping secrets from him. She didn't like being deceitful. Even in a short-term relationship, being honest meant something, and she and Brett had been straightforward with each other so far. Pete seemed to sense her doubt, and his tone turned urgent.

"Please, Lauren. I don't know what's up with you and my brother, but I do know you're only here for a short while, but Graciela and I live here. I'm not asking you to lie, I'm just asking you to...forget what you saw."

Lauren nodded slowly. He had a point. She was only a visitor, and she had no business getting involved in family dramas.

"Sure, Pete, I won't say a word. I can only imagine how much it means to her to have you, considering she's away from her family."

"I know she misses them, and she sends most of what she earns back home."

Lauren was moved by the love and admiration she saw in his eyes, and she reached out, touching his forearm. "She sounds lovely. I have a feeling Brett would be happy for you. Why don't you give him the chance and tell him about you two?"

"You don't know my brother very well, Lauren. He's a great guy, a good man, but he's strictly by the book. And believe me, he doesn't want to hear about my love life. He's got enough on his mind lately with—"

Lauren waited for him to finish his sentence, and prompted him when he remained silent, as if he didn't know what to say next.

"What's Brett been through lately?"

"Uh, just getting the ranch ready for visitors, and you know, he shoulders most of the burden for running the place. I'm more like an assistant manager. Brett runs the whole show. It's just how he is, but he has enough to think about without my problems on top of it."

Lauren also got the distinct feeling that Pete wasn't telling her the whole story.

And again, it wasn't her business.

"I suppose he would tend to take on a lot of responsibilities, seeing that he had to take over so much when your parents died."

A quick shadow passed over Pete's face.

"I'm sorry. I shouldn't have blurted that out. A loss like that must never go away completely."

He shrugged it off. "Nah, it's okay. It's been a long time. Brett really took the harder hit. I was just a kid, and a pain in the ass to boot. I didn't make it easy on him. I think they'd be proud of how the place has come along, though."

"I think you're right."

He cleared his throat, looking around at the stalls. "Hey, you said you came here to learn a little more about horses—do you ride at all?"

She shook her head vehemently. "I've never even

been this close to one before. They're huge. Kinda scary. Do they bite?"

"They can, and sometimes they kick, but not usually. Only if something really spooks them. You get used to them after a while, learn their personalities, which ones you can handle and which ones you're better off leaving for someone else. Once you're around them more, they don't seem so scary."

"If you say so."

"These animals here are all rescue horses—Brett and I have adopted them and retrained them for general use, riding lessons and the like. They're pretty used to being ridden by beginners and have gentle natures, which is why we picked them. The horses down in the other barn are work horses, and some of them need a stronger hand."

"Got it—these are the friendly horses."

Pete grinned. "This one is Macy."

He reached out and ran his hand down the long neck of a beautiful chestnut colored horse. "She's the sweetest girl you could ask for. I think you'd get along fine with her. We use her with kids and she just seems to have some innate understanding of how to behave with people who aren't used to horses."

"She seems very smart. Look at her—the way her ears are perking it's like she understands every word you say."

"Horses are intelligent. Macy has smarts, but she also has gentleness. It's amazing really, considering the shape she was in when we got her. Some asshole, excuse my language, had left her wasting in a dirty barn, and they found her when a neighbor called the sheriff." Pete, obviously still emotional about the issue, shook his head. It fascinated Lauren, how the two brothers were so different, how expressive Pete was compared to Brett's controlled reserve. It made her wonder about the emotions that lay beneath Brett's cool exterior.

"That's horrible," she said.

"The guy had all kinds of animals overrunning the place, all of them sick or hurt. Macy was a bag of bones when we got her. She could have been skittish, difficult—a very few never come back around—but she just didn't go that way. She was perfect from the moment she got here."

"I can't understand how anyone could hurt an animal—especially one as noble as this. It's so good of you to save them."

He looked away, modest, and she smiled. These were two very good-hearted men that she'd been fortunate to meet up with.

"I can show you how to brush her, if you want. It's a good place to start getting comfortable with them. Macy loves to be groomed. She didn't get a lot of TLC in her early years, so the touching soothes her."

Lauren thought about it for a moment, assessing the horse who looked back at her in what seemed to be quiet persuasion.

"That would be awesome. Thanks, Pete."

He turned a gaze on her that seemed a little too serious for his young age. "You're really nice, Lauren. I'm glad my brother bumped into you, even if you are only staying around for a while."

As he turned away, she wondered why suddenly the idea of her short stay bothered her.

BRETT SAT AT HIS DESK, pouring over the books one more time. Something was off, but there had to be an explanation he wasn't seeing. He reviewed the ranch finances once a quarter, and it wasn't a job he particularly enjoyed. It was made even harder by the fact that his concentration was shot. He'd come into his office to focus on work and avoid the curious stares of the ranch staff, and thought that looking over the numbers would help him stop feeling so itchy to get back to Lauren.

Could be having her around was going to be more difficult than he imagined, mostly because all he really wanted to do was go upstairs and get her clothes off and not come back out for a few days.

But that was impossible. He had a business to run, and going over the books should have been a routine job, but there seemed to be mismatches between the amount spent on various ranch supplies and the actual inventory. His accountant took care of things on a regular basis, but Josh was off-site and only crunched the numbers. All of his work was done at his office in Phoenix and he didn't have any knowledge of inventory or what happened on the ranch.

Brett did, however, and the increase in feed and veterinary costs, housekeeping supplies and mechanical services seemed higher than normal. Just slightly, but the increase was there. Sometimes that happened, if there was a sickness running through the animals, or a similar situation. These costs, however, seemed more mysterious. He had no idea what would have caused such uniform increases across the budget.

He'd have to do some checking, but it was possible somebody was making it look like they were ordering supplies, but then pocketing the cash. Josh probably didn't notice because the increased amounts were spread over several categories and so no single amount appeared much out of the ordinary, but taken together, they added up to a couple thousand dollars, at least.

Who would do such a thing? Most of the people who worked the ranch had been there for years, and only a handful of people had authority to order supplies. None of them would hurt the ranch or Brett, but then again, he'd trusted Marsha, too, and look where that had landed him.

Closing the spreadsheets and shutting off his laptop, he pushed away from the desk, the tangy aroma of Davie's tomatillo sauce teasing his senses.

Davie was the most amazing cook; Brett couldn't

have found anyone better if he'd yanked a chef out of a four-star restaurant. In fact, Davie was probably better because he cooked real food that people liked, and plenty of it. When their guests came in off the ranch after a day of activity they were hungry and wanted something with substance, and Davie was creative as well as practical.

However, Davie didn't order his cooking supplies directly, so Brett knew he wouldn't lose his cook to embezzlement charges. That was a huge relief. In fact, Brett had offered Davie his own kitchen account, but he preferred to put in a monthly list of supplies to either Pete, Sherry or Brett. Davie was probably smart for wanting to stay away from the financial side of things.

Deke and Buck were the only two other people who had access to funds, both managing animal costs and other maintenance. Could one of them be ripping him off? Deke had once had a gambling problem, but that had been years ago, and until now Brett had nearly forgotten about it.

He exited the office, and left his suspicions there as well. His stomach rumbled. How quickly the afternoon had passed—it was almost dark outside.

He ambled past Lauren's room and knocked softly at the door. His pulse picked up almost immediately, but there was no answer. He went down into the kitchen where guests were starting to gather, drawn by the temptation of the steaming platters of enchiladas Davie was putting out on the buffet. Lauren wasn't among them.

"Davie, have you seen Lauren?"

His cook glanced up, carrying heavy stoneware bowls of homemade salsa to the tables. "Not since lunch."

Brett said hello to a few of the guests, politely inquiring as to how their days had gone and receiving glowing reports of the ride up into the mountains with Deke. Brett tried to pay attention, but had to excuse himself as smoothly as possible to go find Lauren. He headed to the lower barn and saw Pete coming up to the house.

"Hey, you see Lauren?"

Pete nodded, grinning. "She's down with Macy. I was teaching her how to groom, and once she got started, I couldn't pry her away."

Relief made Brett's step lighter and he chuckled. "Yeah, Macy is a charmer."

"Lauren is a nice woman. Seems like she's afraid of a lot of things. Took a while and a lot of convincing to even get her comfortable standing next to Macy."

Brett wasn't sure how he felt about his little brother spending time with Lauren, or the warmth in his voice when he spoke about her. He checked a little riff of jealously. He was just being touchy because of his lingering insecurities with Marsha.

"She was raised in a city, not on a ranch. Lots of

things here might be intimidating to city people. That's not new."

"I guess. She just reminds me of a skittish horse, you know, one that's been misused a bit."

Brett planted his hands on his hips, eager to make his way down to the barn, and pushing Pete along to his point. "You got something to say, Pete?"

"Just be careful with her, is all. You're not thinking straight, with all that's happened, and you don't want to hurt this woman as you work the mess with Marsha out of your system."

"You're telling me how to handle my women, now?" Brett put the emphasis on *my,* and watched his brother's back stiffen. He and Lauren were adults, and they were clear on what they were doing. It wasn't anyone's business, not even Pete's. Brett didn't mind staking his claim, if only with his brother.

"Maybe it's best if you go up and get some dinner, leave adult things to the adults," he said, still peeved as he turned away, knowing he'd end up apologizing for that one later, but not quite yet. He heard Pete curse as Brett continued toward the barn, ending the conversation. He and Pete were close most of the time, but he wasn't about to take advice on women from his little brother. That was just adding insult to injury.

The horse barn was softly lit by a white light that illuminated the crack between the partly closed doors. No one was around; everyone had hustled off to dinner. All Brett heard as he entered was the shuffling movements of the animals and a gentle humming from somewhere in the back.

Lauren, of course, and a song he recognized but couldn't name. He stood for a moment, listening, his mood shifting almost immediately, the agitation falling away. She had a soothing voice, and he bet she could sing well, if her humming was any sign.

He moved slowly in the direction of her voice, not wanting to startle her, but also not wanting to break the almost magical sense of calm in the barn. Even the horses seemed more relaxed than usual, their indolent gazes following his progress.

He paused about ten feet away. She was grooming Macy with affectionate hands and meticulous care—had Pete said she'd never been around horses before? Brett would not have guessed that from how competently she worked, rubbing down the horse's coat to a chestnut gleam, the fingers of her other hand stroking Macy's neck rhythmically.

Brett had been around horses his entire life, and he knew there were some people, even trained hands, who didn't necessarily have the connection with the animals that made the difference between a good handler and one that could work magic. Inexperienced or not, he was willing to bet that Lauren, with practice, would be incredible with the animals. Macy looked like she was about to melt into a puddle.

"You know, all the rest of them are going to want the same treatment," he said, amused at how she and Macy simultaneously both swung their heads back to look at him. Lauren was surprised, and Macy was annoyed at having her spa treatment interrupted.

She smiled, slightly pink in the cheeks from the exertion of working on the horse, and excitement lit her eyes. Brett smiled widely for no reason, he just felt good looking at her—really good, if the hardening in his jeans was any indication.

"She's so sweet. I was nervous at first, but Pete showed me how to groom her, except for her hooves, and it's just so peaceful. I think I've enjoyed it as much as she has."

"You have a way with it. Not everyone does."

She flushed with pleasure. "I think she's to credit for that, not me. She's so gentle."

Brett pushed off of where he'd been leaning on a post and came over, stroking his own hand down Macy's silky nose.

"Most of them are that way, actually. Some are more spirited, younger, and can get a little randy, but none of them are what I'd call mean. We can't have difficult horses with the guests, or with the work horses, either. They're here to do a job, either way."

"I'd like to do more of this, if it's okay. Maybe tomorrow?"

"You can do whatever you like, just ask me or whoever's around to help you get them out. It's a better idea to latch them out here in the open rather than getting in the stall with them, until you're more comfortable. Also easier not to end up stepping in, uh, getting your shoes messed up."

She grinned. "Thanks. Pete told me these are mostly rescue horses. It's good of you to give them homes, and they deserve a little more love than most, considering what they've gone through before."

Brett, touched, swept his thumb along her cheek. "You have a big heart, Lauren."

"So do you, taking them in."

He didn't know why her words and the warmth in her gaze made him vaguely uncomfortable, but he looked away.

"Would you like to learn to ride?"

"I never really thought about it—six hours ago I would have said no."

"What a difference a day makes. What do you say now?"

She smiled. "Maybe. I'll spend a little more time just getting used to being next to them first. They're kind of intimidating."

"You have Macy here in the palm of your hand. I have a feeling you'd be an excellent horsewoman."

She smiled again, blushing.

"You look pretty when your cheeks flush like that—not that you're not drop-dead gorgeous anyway, but there's something about how you look right now that's turning me on something fierce…"

"Oh, yeah?" Her voice dropped, her tone getting that husky, alluring quality that had knocked him off his feet the night when she'd shown up at his door in that dress. But even now, in jeans and a T-shirt, she had him hornier than a rutting bull, and his gaze dropped to where her nipples hardened against the soft cotton, and he knew he wasn't the only one.

"Yeah."

Taking a second to make sure Macy was securely attached to her post, he grabbed Lauren's hand and led her around the horse to the empty stall behind them. Wasting no time, he had Lauren up against the wall in the shadowed corner faster than the crack of a whip. Desire made him impatient, and she didn't seem to mind, opening her lips for him and arching against him with sinful intent.

"We never seem to make it to dinner," he said breathlessly, laughing against her neck as his hand closed over one breast, caressing her through the thin fabric and feeling the heat of her skin.

"Are you complaining?"

"Hell, no. Who needs food?"

Her hand slid down his stomach to his crotch, giving as good as she got. He groaned in response, realizing, with a twinge of embarrassment that he'd come easily if she kept going. He hadn't been this fast in years, always priding himself on taking his time, going the distance. Isn't that what women wanted? Would she be less than impressed at his current level of excitement?

"You have to stop that, darlin'"

"Why?" She managed to wrap her fingers mostly around him even through the thick fabric of his jeans, and he ground against her, his vision blurring and his mind going blank right along with it.

"A man can only take so much, that's why."

She kissed him lightly, drawing her tongue along his bottom lip, and she didn't stop rubbing, in fact, she picked up her rhythm. *Goddammit, he was close.* He wanted to pull away, but no, he didn't— it was just too good.

"Lauren," he warned on a growl.

"Brett, I'm more than happy to make you come," she teased, dragging her lips down his throat.

"I don't want to come. I mean, I do, but I should take care of you first. This is too fast…"

"Stop trying to boss me," she scolded in a sexy tone. "It's so hot to see you this way, this close to the edge, to know it's because of me…"

He wasn't a fool and his hungry body wasn't giving him much choice anyway, so he did as she asked, giving himself over and pressing hard against her, taking what she was offering. She was sandwiched between his body and the wall, kissing the life from him as he felt himself tighten.

When she deftly moved up and slid her hand down

inside his pants and closed over him, within seconds he shot over the edge so quick and so hard he threw his head back, breaking the kiss and riding out a strong, mind-numbing orgasm. Panting, he leaned in against her, catching his breath.

"I swear to God, Lauren, you turn me inside out…I usually last a lot longer than that…"

"Drop that, will you? I love that I can do that to you…that you didn't hold back…"

He looked into her passion-glazed eyes and knew she was as turned on as he was. Even so, he didn't intend on letting her out of this stall until she experienced exactly the same satisfaction he had. Then he'd make sure to do it again, later, because as cool as she was with his hair-trigger response, he was determined to make sure she knew he had some self-control. He rubbed a thumb over a still-rigid nipple, and felt her shudder.

"You're ready, too, sweetheart, I can feel the heat pouring off of you. I bet you're wet and slick, aren't you?"

He purred in her ear, knowing she liked verbalizing sex. He described exactly what he was going to do to her, and then started to do it when she sagged against him, slack with desire.

"Brett, I need you to touch me…I want you to make me come," she begged prettily, catching her lip in her teeth in a way that he found sexy as hell.

"I plan to, sweetheart, just like you did for me."

The door creaked, and they both froze. Brett hunkered down slightly, lowering Lauren to sit on a square of hay in the corner of the stall, taking them below visibility as two sets of footsteps came toward them. Brett peered up over the edge, seeing Deke and one of the female guests. They stopped about five stalls down, Deke was introducing the woman to a horse she was going to use in a lesson the next day.

He smiled at Lauren, lifting a finger to his lips. She nodded, her cheeks still pink with arousal, her eyes communicating something between frustration and worry at being interrupted.

He wondered if that was necessarily a problem. Meeting her gaze, daring her to respond, he reached over to touch her again, testing her reaction. When his hand closed over her breast, massaging and pulling her nipple to a sharp, hard point, she seemed startled, but didn't make a sound. On the contrary, she closed her eyes and arched into his touch.

It was all the invitation he needed.

6

LAUREN WANTED the satisfaction that only Brett could offer, but she was also intently aware that two other people stood less than twenty feet away from them, talking. What if they came over to Macy to check on why the horse was out of her stall? If Deke and the woman came that close, they'd spot them for sure.

Yet, while her mind shrank at the possibility of being caught, her body responded to the risk with outright abandon. Regardless of her reservations about being caught, she held his gaze as he touched her and silently dared him to do more, letting her knees fall open and inviting him to give her what she needed.

The next minute she was being pressed against a hard length of well-muscled thigh, Brett leaning down to cover her lips in a hot kiss. She moved against him, swallowing the moan that wanted to break free as he pressed harder, tempting her, but she was afraid of them being discovered.

She buried her face in his neck, holding her breath, everything that was building inside of her threatening to explode at any second. Her mind whirled with doubts. They shouldn't be taking these chances…it was too risky for both of them, just for the sake of stealing a few moments of pleasure.

Brett drew back, sensing her mental shift. She started to say something, but he lifted a finger to his lips again to remind her. His gaze was wicked. He was enjoying torturing her in this way. He wasn't worried at all. Quite the opposite. She started to object, but he sent her a warning glance, looking back to where Deke and the woman continued to talk.

When he lowered his head and sucked her nipple through her shirt, biting lightly and sending a blaze of need rocketing through her, she almost cried out. She fought for control. He was making it harder and harder to be quiet, but the restriction of silence was also heightening every sense, intensifying every sensation.

She was held in a sensual clinch, his large hands closing over her backside in such a way that he ground her against his thigh in a rotating, relentless motion that had her hovering on the edge, writhing beneath him to get closer, to have more. She found what she desired as she bucked against him, smothering a sigh against his chest as the orgasm throbbed on and on, leaving her wilted and sweaty, thoroughly satisfied— for the moment.

Her heart picked up speed again, her body craving a more intimate joining as she realized he was still hard. Lauren wanted him inside of her so much she almost wanted to go for it, right here, right now.

They held each other tight for a few minutes, coming back to earth, and she heard the footsteps move away from them, toward the doors. It was finally quiet again, except for the sound of animals.

"I think we're alone."

"But wasn't it fun when we weren't?" he teased, straightened, peering around the barn. She smiled, enjoying this playful side of him that only seemed to emerge when they were alone and intimate. The rest of the time he was so serious and controlled.

"That was wicked, Brett. We could have been caught." She meant to chastise, but caught the edge of excitement still lingering in her voice.

"And that's what made it so much better, didn't it?"

She blushed hot and nodded. "I'm discovering all kinds of things with you. I've never had sex with a stranger, or in a public place, and here I've done both in the space of twenty-four hours."

He smiled as they left the stall, gathered up Macy's ropes and led her back into the stall.

"It's not my normal fare, either." He shook his head, looking at her in a sideways sweep that melted her. "I guess you just bring it out in me."

Lauren felt a zing of something other than lust go through her at his casual admission, and she bent to pick up a few leather straps from the floor to keep her hands busy. What was she feeling? Was it just lust? How could it be anything else? They'd only known each other a day.

Yet, when she was with Brett, it was like she was a different person. One she liked a whole lot more than the old, repressed, boring version of herself. She was also having a hell of a lot more fun.

"What are these?" She held up the straps.

"Lead ropes. I don't know why they're lying there. They should be put away."

She pulled the length of soft, worn leather between her palms and looked at Brett again, reminding herself that experimentation and fun were what this was all about, nothing more.

"If you really feel like experimenting, maybe we could find some creative use for these…"

His eyes narrowed, and he picked up the ropes from the floor, not saying a word. For a moment, she thought she'd gone too far, but when he looked at her, his eyes were hot.

"There are probably some new, clean ones in the inventory. I'll find them."

The rasp of need in his voice triggered a sense of female power she'd never had before, and she feared it could be addictive.

"Sounds like a date."

He nodded, securing the gate on the stall, and handed her the ropes, drawing the straps forward, gently allowing the leather to ride along the inside of her palm before he hung them up on a hook behind him.

"You can count on it, darlin'. But it's about time we joined everyone for dinner."

"Won't it look suspicious, both of us arriving at the same time?"

"No need to sneak around. I made no secret of the fact that I'd gone searching for you."

"I guess I was just thinking you wanted to be discreet, the last half hour aside."

"Sure, but discreet is one thing, and sneaking around is another. I don't want you thinking that I don't want to be seen with you. It's not like that with us, okay? Are you ashamed of what we're doing?"

She looked at him in astonishment. "No, not at all. I'm just thinking, this is your home, your business—"

"Then let me worry about it."

She was getting used to this, how he stated things, short and sweet, and did as he'd asked earlier, to take him at face value. "Well, okay. But I could use a shower."

He looked at her curiously through slightly narrowed eyes, as if still wondering if she were trying to avoid being seen with him, but then he nodded easily. "See you at dinner, then."

Lauren knew this thing between them was only about casual sex, but even so, she liked it when he took her hand in his while they walked. And when they stepped slowly up the front steps, and he opened the door for her, her cowboy gentleman, she tried to ignore the sense of how right it felt as they went inside together.

"WHERE HAVE YOU BEEN? I've been worried sick!" Becky's relief was tangible over the phone, and Lauren immediately felt terrible. She'd completely lost track of life off the ranch.

"I'm so sorry, Beck. I've been forgetting to check my messages. I guess time got away from me. I should have called and told you how things were going."

She looked around the main room of the house. This was the only place her cell phone seemed to hold a signal. Still, Lauren felt uncomfortable taking a personal phone call in the middle of the house, where anyone could be listening in.

"Thanks, I'm just glad to have caught up with you. We have an offer on the house, though there's a problem. When I couldn't get you, I wondered. After all, it's been over a week and the last I knew you'd taken off with a cowboy you'd met on the side of the road."

"On your advice, I might remind you," Lauren said teasingly, and Becky laughed, sounding more relaxed.

"True enough. So how did it go? Where are you? Did you have a good time?"

Lauren ran a hand through her hair. "Uh, yeah. You could say that."

"Ohh…I know that tone of voice. Tell me—what happened? You sound different."

Lauren smiled a little. How could she possibly tell her friend what the last week of her life had been like? She'd completely immersed herself in ranch life and in Brett.

"It went really well. I'm staying at his ranch."

"His ranch? You're still with him? You went home with him? I thought we'd discussed the concept of the one-night stand, but you clearly didn't get the point."

"Stop teasing me. This is his home, but I'm here as a guest. They run a vacation getaway here, and he and I connected, you know, that first night—"

"So you both thought you could extend your playtime a little longer," Becky interrupted. "He was that good, huh?"

Lauren closed her eyes, a montage of passionate moments flickering before her.

"Oh, Becky, you have no idea. I feel like a new person. I love it here. I'm learning to ride horses. I went hiking in the mountains yesterday, and helped make dinner for eighteen people the other night."

"That doesn't sound much like a vacation to me."

Lauren laughed. "Well, you kind of have to be here. But he has a huge Jacuzzi in his room, and that's all I'm sharing on that score."

"Oh, c'mon! Throw me a bone. After everything I've told you over the years—"

"Often too much, I might add."

They laughed. Lauren relented, slightly. "He's great. I'm having a great time with him. He…inspires me to try new things."

"That's intriguing. What kinds of new things?"

"That's all you get," Lauren said with a laugh.

"Buzz kill," Becky grumped. "Okay, but you have something, a tone of voice…you're not falling for this cowboy, are you?"

Lauren blinked, taking a deep breath.

"No. Not at all. Not in the way you mean. I mean, we don't really share much time together except for nights, and then we're not exactly spending our time talking. We don't really know anything about each other. I mean, he knows I'm divorced, but he doesn't know why, or anything else about my life. I don't know much about his life either, except for things on the ranch, so you know, I don't think—"

"Whoa! Okay, you're clearly on a superbabble, which you only do if you're nervous or if you've been holding something in. I'll guess you want more with this guy, but for him, it's only sex, right?"

"Maybe. But it doesn't matter. We had an agreement, and I've gotten no indication he wants to make it more than it is."

"That's probably a good thing. He sounds like a great guy, but he's just your rebound fling. Remember that."

"I don't like how that sounds—he's not that."

Lauren thought of Brett's smile, and his eyes. He was more than a rebound, always would be, even after she left this place. He'd shown her how to be brave again, how to be a woman.

"There's no way he can be anything but—he's the first man you're sleeping with after your divorce, hence, rebound guy. Those flings are great, but they don't last. They're not meant to. Believe me, if you stick around too long, it will crash. And I know you jump into things heart first, but just keep your heart intact here, sweetie. You don't need to get yourself hurt again."

"I'm not going to get hurt."

"Lauren, repeat after me: This is just a fling. Just for fun."

"I am in the middle of the house, Beck. I'm not saying that."

Except for the one hundred times a day she reminded herself of exactly that fact, she thought. It was true that maybe she'd started having some feelings for Brett. When she woke up in the middle of the night, finding herself cradled in his arms, her cheek burrowed comfortably against the crinkly hair on his strong chest, she couldn't help feeling something more than desire.

She hadn't thought about what it was, but what she did know was that no man had ever held her in her sleep like that before. Wes had wanted a large bed, and liked to keep to his side of it, for the most part. Brett wasn't a rebound guy; she refused to think of him that way. However, she didn't know exactly what he was, either, because Becky was right.

"Okay, anyway. Just be careful. Have fun, but this is just the beginning, Lauren. There's a whole new exciting life ahead of you. Remember the Golden Rule: you don't have to fall in love with every guy you sleep with."

"I didn't know that was the Golden Rule, but okay. You said there was an offer on the house…. What's the problem?"

"There was a glitch in the title transfer. You own the house, that's clear in the settlement, but Wes's name still appears on some of the paperwork, and we can't go to closing until he signs off."

"So what's the problem?"

"He's stalling. He's just being a dick, but it could mess up the sale. The buyers need to close. They have an offer on their own home, and we need to do this fast."

"Dammit! What's wrong with him? We're over." She ran her fingers through her hair, agitated again, wishing all these sticky things from her past would just go away for good.

"Yeah, and he's going to make you pay for that. Maybe literally, if we can't get this paperwork through in time. I'm working on it, but we'll see."

"What do you recommend? Do I need to come back?"

Just as she said the words, Brett walked into the room and caught her eye, the questions clear in his expression. He couldn't help but have overheard, but she had to concentrate on what Becky was saying.

"No, there's nothing you can do for the moment, unless he decides to put up a fight, and even then your lawyer and I can act on your behalf. Dragging you back here might be exactly what he's trying to do, and let's not give him the satisfaction. Enjoy your vacation, but keep in touch, okay?"

"Okay," Lauren agreed. "E-mail me if I don't get to my phone, wait, hold on." She looked at Brett, questioning if that was okay since she'd have to use his computer. "I'll check e-mail every morning until I hear something from you," she clarified, finishing up her talk with Becky and setting down the phone with a sigh.

"Thanks. That was my best friend, who also happens to be my real estate agent. I've been so busy here I'd kind of completely forgotten I have things going on back east."

Brett reached out to touch her face, a small, affectionate gesture often shared when they were alone. She was starting to treasure each one.

"That's what vacations are for. Forgetting."

"I suppose. But I do need to keep in contact."

"Is there a problem? I didn't mean to listen in, but I couldn't help but hear something about going back?"

She shook her head. "Well, hopefully I won't

have to. There are some complications with selling the house. It could get messy, and I might have to go back at some point, but not yet."

She felt like she was talking in vague phrases that tried to communicate but didn't say much. It had been a week and she'd shared more intimate things with Brett physically than she had with any other man she'd ever known, but they still knew next to nothing about each other on a personal level.

In fact, she'd picked up some stress from him as well, lately, and had been tempted to ask if everything was okay, or if she could help. But she wasn't sure if she should. The boundaries of their relationship had been clearly drawn.

Becky was right—this was a finite thing, a pleasurable pursuit and nothing more. Brett hadn't made any moves toward sharing with her, either, and she didn't want to freak him out by suddenly demanding more from their relationship than he'd counted on.

"That's good," he murmured, stepping closer. "I worried for a moment that I might have to say goodbye sooner than I'd counted on."

He lowered his lips to hers and she responded to the familiar warmth of his kiss, her heart aching a little because his comment confirmed that he was still contemplating that they would part ways eventually.

"I don't want to leave yet, either," she admitted,

more emotion churning inside than she was happy about, hoping he mistook the hoarseness of her voice for desire instead of anything deeper.

She poured herself into the kiss, focusing on how tightly he wrapped his arms around her back, his fingers massaging the tense muscles along the column of her spine and lower back, sore from riding lessons the entire afternoon before. His hands were heaven.

"Excuse us," a biting voice cut between them like a sharp blade, and though she stepped back suddenly, Brett didn't release her right away. In fact, he took his time, even sliding his hand down to squeeze hers before letting go. That stubborn streak was also something she was starting to see as she got to know him better.

Still, she felt inexplicably guilty as she met Sherry's furious gaze. She stood in the doorway with a man who appeared to be extremely uncomfortable. Lauren could relate.

"What is it, Sherry?" Brett sounded cool and collected, and maybe not entirely happy with his manager. Tension boomeranged around the room. Sherry didn't seem the least bit intimidated, meeting her boss with the same offended expression.

"Mr. Lawson is here for his appointment regarding the accounting. He'd been waiting for fifteen minutes, so we came to find what was…detaining you," she explained, her gaze swinging back to Lauren, who shifted uncomfortably.

Brett let go of her hand, and in the middle of the desert afternoon, she thought she felt a chill. Lauren had the rare urge to wipe the satisfied smirk off Sherry's face.

"Mr. Lawson, I'm sorry to keep you waiting. Give me a minute and we'll go to my office and I can show you what I need help with."

The man seemed agreeable enough, and happy to be excused from the awkward situation.

"Why have you brought him here?" Sherry asked Brett, ignoring Lauren for a moment. "Are we being audited? Is there some kind of problem?"

"Don't worry about it. Just an irregularity in the books I wanted a second opinion on."

"But—"

"Sherry, thanks, could you excuse us for a moment?"

Brett's request was polite, but Lauren could see from the way Sherry's back stiffened that she didn't take well to being shut out, not one bit.

Brett walked back to Lauren, planting a kiss on her forehead. "Sorry about that."

"I don't think Sherry likes me being here very much—I suspect she might have a thing for you."

Brett looked shocked. "Sherry? Hardly. She's happily married with grandkids on the way. Why would you think that?"

"I don't know. It's the only thing that makes sense. She's been angry with me since the moment I stepped in the house—she's clearly possessive of you." She held her hands up, regretting that her mouth had run away with her thoughts. "I'm sorry to mention it— I don't want to start anything or get her in trouble. Or overstep my bounds."

"Don't worry, you're not. I don't think it's me as much as the ranch. She's been here almost as long as we have, Pete and me, that is. There are some other things bothering her, I know, that have nothing to do with you."

"Like what?"

"Personal stuff."

Lauren tried to ignore the little sting his short reply elicited, relating for a brief moment to how Sherry felt—when Brett closed an avenue of conversation, he did so with finality. She forced a smile, determined not to sulk.

"Forget I mentioned it?"

"Sure—I'd forgotten about the meeting, too, actually. I was coming up here to try to catch you."

"What for?"

"Well." He planted another soft kiss on her cheek, making her shiver down to her toes, erasing the hurt of the moment before. "I thought it might be fun to take the day off tomorrow and do something together, spend the day."

"Sounds fun."

"Good." He headed for the office and paused, looking back at her with that slight smile she loved.

"You know, I don't even know what your favorite color is."

Lauren's heart swelled. *Don't read too much into it*, her head warned. But her heart won out. He wanted to get to know her better. He wanted more than sex.

"It's moss green."

He nodded, and disappeared down the hall.

Lauren watched him walk away, an excitement she hadn't felt for a very long time grabbing hold of her. She could hardly wait to see what tomorrow would bring.

7

"YOU'RE SITTING PRETTY well for a newbie," Brett teased, assessing Lauren's posture as they approached a shady spot near a pair of towering rocks. She looked better than good on the horse, her back straight, her slender form moving in concert with Macy in a way that made him think of sex...which wasn't a surprise. Everything about Lauren made him think of sex.

"Thanks. I love it, and Macy makes it easy."

"She's really taken to you."

She patted the horse's mane, and took a deep breath, glancing around.

"Are we stopping here?"

"Just up past these rocks. Remember the naturally occurring pools I mentioned? I wanted to show you the one I keep to myself."

"Keep to yourself?"

"Well, if anyone else knows about it, I've never seen them here. I come here to think, to get away when I need to."

"And are you sure you want to share it with me?"

"Absolutely. You up for a longer ride?"

"Yes. I think most of the soreness from the first few days has lessened, or I'm just so used to it that it feels normal." She laughed, and he did, too.

"It's just another twenty minutes up—a little steep, but Macy will know how to maneuver the trail, so you can just let her follow me."

"Okay."

They wound up around the path curling through the sand, scrub and rocks, and Brett's soul eased as he spotted a familiar thatch of trees right before the pool.

He'd never brought anyone here, it was his secret place. It was where he'd come as a child to be alone, and then later on, where he'd spent many hours after his parents had died. Never once had he wanted anyone else to share the spot with him, but with Lauren, it felt right.

A lot of things were feeling right these days, most of them having to do with Lauren, which was a problem, considering she was taking off at some point, maybe sooner than later. That was their original deal, but it wasn't enough…for him at least, not anymore.

So he decided to ask her to spend the day with him. He'd been fairly sure she might be receptive to him saying he wanted more than a fling before he'd walked in on that phone call. Now he wasn't so sure.

She had a life, a past that he knew nothing about. All he really knew about her was that she was divorced and great in bed. At least she knew something about his family, his home. He was at a distinct disadvantage, especially concerning his own personal secrets. What would she think if she found out about Marsha, about the wedding, and about the whole damned mess? He cursed silently, wishing he could avoid the whole thing.

He couldn't get a fix on how she was thinking or feeling except that she seemed to be enjoying their time together as much as he was. If he only knew how she felt, or if he could learn more about her, maybe he could risk telling her about Marsha. Or maybe it was best to leave things be—they were having a great time, enjoying each other—why muddy the waters with complications? They'd go their separate ways and enjoy the memory.

"Oh my God…look at that. It's like something out of a movie," Lauren exclaimed as they broke through the trees.

The rocky edges of the main canyon surrounded the pool at the bottom. Its black, warm depths glittered in the sunlight.

"The water is around one hundred or so degrees," Brett said.

"It's a hot spring?"

He nodded. "They're all over the southwest, some are popular tourist destinations. I thought about opening this one to guests, but I couldn't bring myself to do it."

"I don't blame you. How deep is it?"

He shrugged. "Don't know. Damned deep. You swim? If not, there are some ledges where you can sit and be mostly under the water."

"I swim. Lessons from the time I was a toddler. I didn't bring a suit, though."

He caught her eye, his own desire spiking again. "No need for one. No one's around here, just us two."

The color moved up into her cheeks, but she grinned. "Another first—I've never skinny-dipped before."

"Sounds like you led a pretty sheltered existence," he said, hoping she might elaborate, but she just nodded and gazed back at the pool. "Anyway, I had lunch packed. What do you say we eat and then swim?"

She looked apprehensively at the wide rocks that surrounded the pool. "Are there snakes up there?"

"Good chance, this time of day. Don't worry, I'll go first, keep an eye out. If we're careful, it's not a problem. I've seen hundreds of snakes in my life, never been bitten once."

"Once would be enough, I think."

He shrugged. "True, it can be nasty. But don't worry—I won't let anything get you," he promised with a smile, meaning it.

Dismounting from their horses, they left them to rest in the shade.

"There's a nice flat expanse of rock in the shade

right there. I'll grab the food, and let's see what Davie packed. I'm hoping there was enough of that fire-grilled turkey you two made yesterday left for sandwiches."

"It was wonderful, wasn't it? I never would have thought of having turkey like that. Davie is an amazing cook. He said he was trying out that recipe for the *Día de los Muertos* barbeque party?"

"Yeah. He loves that—part of his heritage—but we make it a big deal on the ranch since we don't do much for Halloween, and guests seem to enjoy celebrating the Day of the Dead on the first two days of November with the traditional processions, art, music, dancing and, of course, food, and lots of it."

"I'd heard of it, but I don't really understand it. Sounds kind of morbid."

"Not really. Especially in the desert, and on ranches, you deal with life and death all the time. Surviving hard conditions, dealing with animals. It's around us constantly. The two-day celebration is a way of honoring the dead, people special to us, but it's also a way of recognizing the continuity between life and death—two sides of the same coin, can't escape it."

Lauren mulled that over. "I've never lost someone, not directly. I guess it scares me a little. I can't imagine what you went through losing your parents."

He nodded, sitting back.

"It was tough. But that's why it's so important to

remember, and to celebrate what was good. Davie also puts on a hell of a barbeque. Pete found him cooking at a greasy spoon down on the highway, and after eating the lunch Davie had made, Pete hired him on the spot. I wasn't sure about it until Davie made dinner the first night, and then I was sold. He's been with us ever since," he said, turning away from the subject of his parents and back to his cook.

"Was he a local?"

Brett grabbed a soda and looked up at her briefly. "If that's a nice way of asking if he's legal, yes, he is. I know illegal aliens handle a lot of important work in the area. They do a lot of manual labor that wouldn't get done otherwise, and it benefits everyone. But at the same time, we're having problems with illegals on the land, wrecking stuff, ending up dead, or killing animals. I had three good dogs shot last year."

"Who would do such a thing?"

"Illegals or guides taking them over the border sometimes kill anything that gets in their way or might signal their presence."

Lauren frowned, obviously disturbed.

"I have sympathy, but I like to run everything on the straight up, and frankly, some of them are worse off, or as bad, here as they were in Mexico."

"How do you know the people working for you, like Davie, are legal?"

"All the employees fill out payroll info, including social security or green card information—if they're missing any of that, we don't hire them. Not on my ranch anyway—too many problems come with it."

"Sounds like a good policy," Lauren said and then suddenly was quiet.

He was, too. The conversation brought back the worries he'd pushed to the side for the day, the accountant who'd come out to the ranch the other day confirming his fears, that someone was pilfering money. He'd taken copies of everything, and Brett was conducting his own inventory. They'd find out what was going on, and who was responsible, and then he'd deal with it. But it wasn't what he wanted to think about right now. He found the sandwiches, and laid them out with other goodies Davie had packed.

"This looks delicious. I'm starving," she declared, taking a big bite out of her sandwich.

He liked watching everything she did, including eating, and shook his head. Man, was he heading for trouble. He'd never been fascinated by a woman eating a turkey sandwich before. After munching in companionable silence for a while, he tried to strike up another conversation.

"So, when's your birthday?"

She looked up, a little surprised. "February. Why?"

"Just curious. How old will you be?"

She wrinkled her nose. "Don't you know women hate that question?"

"Yeah, I just never know why. Like my Dad always said, getting older is better than the alternative."

She grinned, and ripped a grape from the bunch sitting between them, bouncing it off his forehead. "Fine. I'll be thirty. The big three-oh. Satisfied?"

"I had that turning point several years ago. It's really not the end of the world."

Sitting back on the rock, she stretched out, tilting her face up into the sun, her hair falling back and her chest arching upward in a way that made Brett forget about lunch. She kept her eyes closed as she responded.

"I know, I know. I guess I just pictured my life differently. I was married, we had a business. It was my life. I thought about having more by now and instead I'm just starting over. Back to scratch."

"By 'more' do you mean children?"

She paused for a moment. "Kids would have been nice, eventually. Of course, all things considered…"

"It would have just made it harder to get out?"

"That and my ex, well…now that I know more about him, he isn't the kind of man I would have wanted to be a father to my children."

"Why?"

Another long pause. She sat up, crossing her legs in front of her and sending him a level look.

"You don't want to hear about all that."

Leaning back on his elbow he stared over at her, hoping he wasn't pushing too hard. "Actually, I do."

She shrugged, then glanced away from him toward the spring. It was a habit he'd observed, how she would find some focal point other than the person she was talking to when she was dealing with something that made her uneasy. Maybe she was afraid her expression would reveal more than she wanted.

It didn't matter. He could tell from her posture that this wasn't easy. Still, he needed to know. He had to trust they had more between them than sex before he could feel comfortable sharing his own secrets.

"Well, okay." She blew out a breath as if gearing up for her explanation, and he felt guilty that his questions were making her so uncomfortable. He moved over, sitting behind her and settling her back against his chest, trying to make her feel safe.

"My ex-husband's name was Wes. I met him when I wasn't even out of college yet. He worked for my dad. He swept me off my feet, my parents loved him, and so we got married."

Brett was taken aback at her dispassionate reciting of fact, especially the last part. "You got married because your parents loved him? What about you?"

"I thought I did, too, but I was too young, and too sheltered to really know anything, let alone what love really is. I'd never even slept with anyone else. I was an only child, and to say I was overprotected doesn't begin to describe how my parents raised me. They loved me to a fault, really. I don't blame them, they're good people, but it was why I didn't know much about the ways of the world, I think. I was so afraid of disappointing them."

"Hmm," he murmured and found a tense spot at the base of her neck, working on it rhythmically.

"Anyway, I was so used to pleasing them that was probably part of it, too. Wes really was charming, and so I got caught up in it. If he had been a different kind of man, maybe it would have worked out. You know, like those arranged marriages where people learn to love each other by being married, and make a life just being together."

"What do you mean, if he were a different kind of man? What kind of man is he?"

He felt her muscles tense.

"He was…possessive. Extremely. To cut a long story short, I found over time he was isolating me from everyone but him. If I even left the house on my own, without him knowing every detail, he would fly into a rage."

"Jesus, Lauren," Brett whispered and slipped his arms around her, drawing her back against him to comfort her. "Did he…did he hit you?" Brett could barely make himself ask, knowing the answer would cut if it were true. Men who hit those smaller or weaker weren't men. Thinking about Lauren in that situation made him sick.

"No, not that. He was…intimidating. He got rough a few times near the end, and that's when I knew I had to get out. I think he might have very possibly become violent had I stayed."

"He doesn't sound like the kind of guy who would just let you go. Is that why you had to leave? Are you running from him?"

Her hair brushed against his cheek when she shook her head. "No, he didn't take it well, but that's not why I left. My dad and mom stood with me, and my dad, well, let's just say he has a lot of business connections in the area, and if there was anything more important to Wes than controlling me, it was succeeding at business. So when my father stepped in, he backed off."

"Good for your dad. He should have squashed him like a bug."

"He wanted to, but all I wanted was out. I think Dad felt guilty on one hand for introducing us, and wanted to keep protecting me on the other. In a way, I suppose I'm grateful for it all, because it's showing me how to make my own decisions, and to get my own life."

"I imagine you were doing that all along. You had the brains to see a problem and leave."

"True. I left because I needed to be on my own, but being so smothered by Wes made me aware of a larger problem. Even though I love my parents, I had to get away from them, too. That probably sounds awful."

Play the *Lucky Hearts* Game

and get...

2 FREE BOOKS and
2 FREE MYSTERY GIFTS...
YOURS to KEEP!

yes! I have scratched off the silver card.
Please send me my *2 FREE BOOKS* and
2 FREE mystery GIFTS. I understand that I
am under no obligation to purchase any books
as explained on the back of this card.

Scratch Here!
then look below to see
what your cards get you...
2 Free Books & 2 Free
Mystery Gifts!

351 HDL ENSL   151 HDL ENZL

FIRST NAME   LAST NAME

ADDRESS

APT.#   CITY

STATE/PROV.   ZIP/POSTAL CODE   (H-B-08/07)

Twenty-one gets you
2 FREE BOOKS and
2 FREE MYSTERY GIFTS!

Twenty gets you
2 FREE BOOKS!

Nineteen gets you
1 FREE BOOK!

TRY AGAIN!

"No, I can see where you're coming from. They want to protect you, but at some point they have to let go. Or you have to make them let go—not fun."

She nodded. "Exactly. They'd have fits seeing me here, on horseback, driving these roads." She laughed softly. "But I love it. I'm discovering so many new things about myself, especially with you."

"I guess that's the point of an adventure, right?"

"Yeah. Now if I can just finish up selling the house, I can really be free," she said, exhaling heavily again, and leaning back against him in a way that made him close his eyes and just soak in the moment.

"Was that the problem with the house? Is Wes getting in the way?"

"Trying to. He's tying up some paperwork, probably in hopes that I'll have to come back. Hopefully Becky and my lawyer can handle it. I know it sounds cowardly, but I want to leave it all behind, to never have to see him again."

"If you have to go, I could go with you. You wouldn't have to face him alone," Brett said, the words spoken before he even knew he was thinking them, startling him as much as her. She turned to gaze at him.

"Why would you do that?"

Cornered. He'd gotten lost in the moment and his mouth had taken the lead. He also meant it—he *would* go with her, if she needed him.

"If you need me, I want to be there, I guess. It

drives me crazy to think someone treated you like that. I'd be happy to knock him flat if it came down to it."

He heard himself and cringed. She might think that she'd escaped one crazy bastard of a husband and bumped into yet another overly protective male, and he held his breath. She touched his face affectionately.

"Thank you. Just knowing you mean that helps me. I could go back and fight my own battles if I have to, but hopefully it will resolve itself. I'd much rather be here with you."

He felt the closeness building between them, and it was disconcerting. Is this what he'd been looking for when he wanted to take her out here? He hadn't thought so, but it felt right.

Brett knew he'd have to share some of his own dirty laundry with Lauren soon, because what they had was clearly more than a fling. Was he up for that? Before he could think too much, he noticed her eyes sweeping over him, a smile lighting her expression.

"What?" he asked.

"You. This is the first time I've seen you all decked out in your cowboy clothes."

"You make it sound like a Halloween costume, Connecticut." He used the teasing nickname gruffly, but there was a smile in his eyes. "These are working clothes, woman."

"I've noticed the guys around the ranch dress that way, but this is the first time I've seen you in the same outfit."

He sighed. "I got up early this morning, before you, sleepyhead, and went out to help with some fence work."

"I know. You're usually gone in the morning when I wake up."

"It's life around here."

"I know. I went to a rodeo once and saw the cowboys all dressed up, but never saw one up close and personal," she teased, and watched his eyes warm.

"Well, that's a show. All these clothes have a function."

She popped to her feet, smiling down at him. "Tell me."

He stood, and as he did, his spurs made a noise, and she started there.

"Why do you wear those? I thought they were just out of the movies. Don't you think they're kind of mean to the horse?"

He rolled his eyes. "These are Garcias, and they're not mean at all if you use them right, to nudge, not to dig. We don't give them to new riders until you learn the basics, but you'd want to wear them, eventually, depending on the horse you're riding, and what you want them to do."

"Hmm. How do they come off?"

He peered at her for a second, then bent down,

unbuckling the strap that held the spur onto his low-heeled boot. Picking them up, he dangled them from his fingers. "Just so."

"What about this?" She tugged on the blue fabric stuffed in his pocket.

"Bandana? We work hard, it's hot. You do the math."

"Back home guys wear them at the gym."

She laughed at the mock-withering look he gave her, and took the bandana, putting it in her own pocket.

"And these. Chaps, right?" She slid her fingers between the top edge of the dusty leather and his jeans, moving them across his lower abs, peeking up at him from under her lashes. "What purpose do these have?"

"Protection, mainly—when we're out on the fences, or anything else around here, it can be dangerous. I got a leg full of thorns once so they're worth the trouble."

"Seems like a lot of extra clothing in his heat—maybe you should take those off, too."

The suggestion in her voice hit home, and he held her gaze.

"Maybe you should help."

She didn't lose time and when the same was done with his shirt, jeans, and boots, she brought herself up near to him, loving how he stood there, unabashed, nearly naked, and not batting an eye. Brett was gorgeous. Sculpted and tan, just looking at him turned her inside out.

"What about your hat?"

He shook his head. "Hat stays on. A man's hat is a personal thing, Lauren."

"What's it made of? It looks different than mine."

"Yours is straw, this is palm leaf."

"I saw other hats in your room. Do they have different uses?"

He nodded and sucked in a breath as she ran her hands over his shoulders, and leaned in to plant a kiss on his chest, right over his heart.

"Yeah, dress, rain, not that we get a lot of that here. I have a lot of hats, but this one is my favorite. My dad bought it for me."

"Where'd you get the tattoo?" She'd been dying to ask every time she'd see the brand at the back of his shoulder.

"College," he said shortly, burying his face in her neck and starting to unbutton her shirt. Within seconds, she was as unclothed as he was, everything except for her hat.

"What did you study? Oh," she gasped as his hands kneaded her breasts, turning the tables on her as he took over their seduction.

"Business management."

"For the ranch," she observed breathlessly as her blood turned hot, and she started to lose track of the conversation, though she badly wanted to know these things about him, just as he had asked about her.

"Yeah." He nipped the tender skin at her shoulder, peering up as the sun moved over them. "We should get in the shade. You'll burn in this sun."

He took off both their hats and placed them carefully on a branch, and she squealed as he picked her up, carrying her over to a spot where the ledge dipped gradually into the black waters of the pool. As the water surrounded her skin, she sighed and relaxed against him. He loosened her arms, and she drifted just inches away from him.

"This is wonderful," she said, enveloped in the warm mineral waters. A thin sheen of perspiration coated her face, and she submerged, letting the wet heat surround her, before emerging again. When she did, the air actually felt cool, which was amazing.

Brett swam easily through the middle of the pool, finding a resting spot on a long jutting rock, hauling himself up. Her breath caught at the play of muscles, the water sluicing off his back and down his backside and powerful, lean legs. It was almost primordial, watching him rise from the water like that. She followed, drawn to him.

She wanted *more.* More of Brett, more of whatever was between them. Oh, it might be the stupidest thing she could do, and maybe a bigger mistake even than Wes had been, because this one she could only blame on herself. She couldn't blame it on being young and stupid, or on trying to please her parents, or anything else.

Brett had been so strong and understanding when

she'd told him about Wes. He hadn't critiqued her or offered platitudes, he'd just been there. A reassuring presence, he'd listened, and she'd felt his own body tense along with hers when she'd told him the worst of it. They hardly knew each other, but wasn't this a man worth getting to know?

She swam over to the rock where he was spread out, his naked body blanketed by a few inches of water. A few bees buzzed around at the corner of the pool, but didn't seem to care about their presence.

Not saying a word, she lifted herself up over the rock and straddled him. Smiling at him with wicked abandon, she teased his cock, sliding back and forth over him until he was hard and jutting upward, eager and hungry for her, eddies of warm water swirling hot around them. He started to sit up, to take control, but she shook her head, putting her hand on his shoulder.

"No. Stay there. Lie back."

He obeyed, propping himself up on his elbows, keeping his head above the water and watching her with hot, expectant eyes. Her clit drifted over the ridge of his erection, the enormous pulse of pleasure caused by the motion pulling a moan from deep inside of her. She heard his gasp as she teased him some more, chasing the wonderful sensations caused by the warmth of the water gushing between her legs and the hardness of his body underneath it all. Bracing her hands on the stone around them to lever herself, she raised and lowered, taking him deep in one delicate plunge, murmuring appreciation as he slid his palms underneath her knees, protecting her.

A breeze wafted between the boulders, caressing her wet skin and making her shiver as she set the rhythm, the cooler air brushing over her breasts and face, her nipples puckering at its touch.

"Lauren, we're not protected," he ground out, his jaw clenched with arousal.

She froze, his body still deeply inside of hers. Her muscles clenched around him instinctively though neither of them moved, and he cursed. For whatever reason, it turned her on even more.

Hell, she'd been so carried away she'd completely forgotten. Burning through the fog of desire in her brain, she mentally figured where she was in her cycle, and smiled down at him.

"I'm okay if you are…"

"We shouldn't take chances," he said regretfully, trying to pull away. Her legs had become much stronger from riding, and she braced over him, his length buried deep inside of her.

"I was married for seven years, Brett, and I never used any kind of birth control after the ceremony except for the calendar. I know my body. It's okay. Trust me."

"As my dad used to say, a lot of babies were born on 'trust me'." His voice was strained. "Neither of us wants that."

"No, but it won't be a problem." She leaned down over him, pressing the hard points of her nipples to his chest, whispering against his mouth, "I promise it will be okay."

He wanted to give in, but she also knew he was a man who took his responsibilities seriously, maybe too seriously. In fact, she wanted to make him let go. It was incredibly important for him to trust her, she realized, to trust her with himself as she had with him, so many times. The war waged inside of him; she could see it on his face. She paused above him, holding her breath.

That held breath was pushed out of her in a delighted gasp as he arched up, driving deeper into her, giving in. Full of desire and joy, she moved faster over him, taking every bit of what she needed and more and came fast and hard, taking him with her, their cries of satisfaction echoing through the canyon surrounding them.

Collapsing on top of him, she met his lips in a kiss, trying to stem the urge to say words that it was far too soon to say. For now, she thought, easing back into the warm waters with him, this was enough.

8

IT WAS SATURDAY NIGHT, and Brett checked himself out once more in the mirror, feeling like a high school kid going out on his first date. In a lot of ways, this *was* his first real date with Lauren. They never made it out to dinner that first night, he remembered with a smile, and the picnic a few days before didn't count, though both were memorable.

This time they were dressing up and stepping out. Saturday and Sunday were Davie's days off, so everyone left the ranch for dinner or fended for themselves. Typically, a bunch of guys from the ranch picked up their girls—or picked up some girls—and met at a small roadside dive called the Desert Rocks Tavern. What the place lost in curb appeal, it made up for in live music and food. Dusty and ramshackle on the outside, on Saturday nights the roadhouse rocked with some of the best local bands, serving up beer and some of the best Tex-Mex around.

It was an experience mostly enjoyed by locals, since out of towners probably wouldn't have the nerve to set foot in the place. However, while every now and then a fight broke out, for the most part everyone just went there for a good time, and that was exactly what he was planning to show Lauren.

He hadn't been to Desert Rocks in years. Marsha never liked the place, and on Saturdays she preferred to drive into the city for a fancy dinner or show. He'd sat through more lame dinner conversation between Marsha and her city friends than he could stand. He hadn't been interested, and they had returned the favor, tagging him the silent cowboy who probably didn't understand their discussion about whatever play or concert they'd gone to see.

Sometimes he'd been relieved when she'd gone by herself, and he took the opportunity to read or get some work done. Had Marsha been out on the town, screwing around on him even then? He hoped Howie was the first, feeling another punch in the gut. Shaking his head, he packed the negative thoughts away. Didn't matter now, over and done.

Tonight he was happy, excited to be going out and excited it was with Lauren.

He was as ready as he could be. Freshly showered and shaven, he wore his black Wranglers, black western shirt, his best hat and comfortable boots for some dancing if Lauren was up for it. He felt more like himself, more lighthearted, than he had in a long while.

The demands of the ranch, losing his parents, raising Pete, and then Marsha, so many things had stolen his attention that the years had flown by and he didn't realize how serious he'd become, how distant from the lighter things in life. Lauren was reminding him how to enjoy it all again.

He liked to dance, and he hoped she did, because it would give him one more opportunity to hold her, and to watch her come out of the carefully constructed shell she'd so obviously lived in for most of her life. The woman who boldly seduced him outdoors at the spring, or the one who was becoming a better horsewoman every day, that was the real woman underneath all those layers of self-protection. He wanted to see more of her.

Lots more.

The sex between them was better than he ever imagined sex could be, more intense, more daring. Still, what was between them was becoming more physical. Brett knew he was looking for something deeper.

It was exactly why he had to tell her about Marsha, and hope she'd understand the reason he'd kept it to himself. It was also why he wanted to ask her not to leave. They needed time to explore and to find out if it was right.

But first, there was fun to be had.

He grabbed his keys and a box from the dresser and headed down the hall to her room. He wanted her in *his* room, in *his* bed—every night—not down the hall. That would begin tonight, he thought to himself resolutely, with a twinge of desire.

Outside the door he raised his hand to knock, but it opened before he could complete the task. She smiled when she saw him.

"Oh! Hi. Good timing." Turning around once, she wiggled her backside flirtatiously and peered over her shoulder at him, her eyebrows raised. "What do you think? I went into town with Davie yesterday, he had to buy some things, so I went shopping and picked this up. The woman at the store helped me find what I needed."

He looked her up and down—slowly—liking what he saw. The soft, expensively faded jeans she wore hugged her curves. A pink spaghetti string top hinted at the delicious cleavage without exposing too much. A fine silver chain with a single, small diamond sat in the hollow of the milky skin of her throat, and he wondered who gave it to her. As his eyes traveled down, though, his smile stretched widely.

"Those are some boots, Lauren." He took in the way the buffed rose leather fit over shapely calves and found himself getting hard thinking about having her wearing nothing but those boots—and her hat.

"Tony Lama Stingrays. I fell in love with them on sight, and decided to splurge. I thought they'd be stiff, but they're really very comfortable. I think I'll be wearing them a lot."

"That's what they're for."

"I could become a boot addict," she warned.

"You wear them well. You stay close to me to-night—can't have you looking like that and being out of eyeshot."

Her cheeks turned pink, and he knew he'd said the right thing.

"You look pretty slick yourself," she said, giving him the same slow once-over he'd given her. "What's in the box?"

Damn, he'd been so taken with looking at her he'd forgotten he was holding the thing.

"Just a little something."

He handed it to her, and smiling at him, she lifted the lid and gasped in delight—at least he thought it was delight as she took the white hat from the box.

"This is for me?"

"I thought you needed your own. I took the liberty of shaping it for you, but you can mess with it, I'll show you how."

"I love the thin black band, how pretty this little decoration on the front is. Is this real silver?"

He nodded and cleared his throat. "Yeah, the conch button is antique, the band is woven from horsehair. It came off my mother's hat. It was her favorite."

Her eyes widened, taking in the import of his words. "Oh Brett. I love this, but I can't take some-thing of your mother's. I love the hat, but maybe you should keep the band."

He shook his head resolutely. "It's just been sitting in the closet all these years. I wear my dad's now and then, but no one's used hers. Her hat wouldn't fit you, but the band is perfect for that hat. I know she'd love for you to have it. She would have liked you—I just have that feeling."

She looked away and he thought she either felt uncomfortable or was getting teary, but when she lifted her head, the emotion in her smile set him back a few steps.

"Thank you. It's one of the most special gifts I've ever received. I'll treasure it always."

She threw the box in the room behind her and plopped the hat on her head. Chuckling, he helped her adjust it just so.

"Perfect," he announced, hoping that later on, Lauren might model that hat and those boots for him when they were all alone.

To say Lauren felt out of her element was putting it mildly, and Brett held her arm tightly linked in his as they entered the broken-down roadhouse. He deftly navigated their path through crowds of people dancing and drinking. The music was blasting loud enough to tempt her to cover her ears. Brett walked up to the bar and shouted an order to a bartender without asking her what she wanted, which was fine since she probably wouldn't have heard him anyway. He handed her an icy bottle of beer

with a glass, and they headed over to the wall farthest away from the band that was just finishing its
song and announcing a break. Lauren's eardrums
sighed with relief.

Brett appeared in his element, pausing to talk with
several men and women in the crowd, and seem-
ingly oblivious to the blatant curiosity in their eyes
when he introduced her. Lauren didn't think much of
it, figuring she was just the new girl in town, and that
was bound to draw some interest. Shrugging it off,
she hung by Brett and smiled when his long, warm
fingers wrapped around hers, and they swooped in
to grab a table just as the current diners vacated.

"Whew, this place is packed! I never would have
guessed, from the looks of the outside," she admitted,
glancing around the room.

"Yeah, it's our best kept secret. They like to discourage tourists."

"Why?"

"Just how they want it. They're always packed,
so who's arguing?"

Lauren shrugged. Thanks to the recent state ban
restricting indoor smoking, the place was smoke-
free and filled only with conversation, laughter, the
pungent scent of beer, bodies, and something spicy
and wicked that she realized was coming from the
table behind them.

"I'm starving," she said, the aroma making her
mouth water.

"I have ribs on order, and some fries—that's what smells so good. They're the best here. The smokers and the pit are outside in a separate shack out back."

"I can feel my cholesterol rising the way I've been eating lately. I'd better be careful or these jeans won't fit in a week," she joked.

"You're probably a lot more active than usual, as well. And I think those jeans fit just right," he added, delivering her a slow, sexy look that had her shifting in her chair at the sudden flash of heat zapping through her. His thumb caressed the center of her palm, and she thought she might melt into a puddle. Then the movement suddenly stopped.

"Well, now, that's interesting."

If the band were playing, she would never have heard him, his voice was so soft, almost as if he were talking to himself. Following the path of his gaze, she saw what had drawn his attention, and felt her own heartbeat pick up a little.

Pete—and Graciela. Standing close together in a shadowed corner, beers in hand. Not realizing they were being watched, Pete had planted a firm kiss on the girl's lips, and the chemistry between them would be obvious to anyone watching.

"I thought Pete had been acting a little strangely lately. I guess that explains it. He's in love—again," Brett said, taking another drink of his beer.

Should she let him know she knew, or play dumb? Lauren went with the latter.

"Is that Pete's girl?"

"One of them. She's also a ranch employee, in housekeeping."

Lauren frowned. She'd had no impression of Pete as a womanizer, and believed he really was in love with Graciela. Of course, she couldn't really tell Brett that—she'd promised Pete she wouldn't.

"Is there a rule against that? Employees dating?"

Brett shook his head. "Not really, but it's something I discourage, especially when it comes to the men who manage the place dallying with housekeepers. Sexual harassment cases don't just happen in the office these days. Not to mention the possibility for accidents at work if the staff aren't focusing on their jobs."

"Pete seems on top of things," she said, hazarding an opinion, and he nodded.

"He is, generally. I always appreciated him coming back from school to help out with the place. He didn't have to. He could have left, and I would have been fine."

"He clearly loves it as much as you do—it's in your blood."

"It is. But he takes risks that make me worry—he doesn't always think first."

"How so?"

"Like this thing now with Graciela. At best, I could lose a good employee or have her looking for a break because she has an in with the boss. At worst, who knows?"

"Give him some credit. He might really like her, and he wouldn't do things to purposely hurt the ranch, right?" Lauren asked the question kindly, catching the lines of worry in his expression.

"Maybe. He knows better, though."

"We all do things against our better judgment, Brett, especially when it comes to the opposite sex," she said softly, and was relieved when he smiled. "You've had a lot of responsibility dropped on you over the years, and you've handled it admirably. But you take things a little too seriously sometimes. Pete's a good man. I think you can relax a little," she said, hoping she wasn't stepping over the line.

He looked her in the eye and she felt like he was staring straight through to her soul.

"Maybe you're right," he said thoughtfully. The next moment, his smile returned and the steaming plates of ribs and fries arrived.

Over their dinner, Lauren ignored the calories she was consuming and enjoyed the food and the company. She even enjoyed the music, once she'd adapted to the loudness, and clapped along with the rhythm, tapping with the beat as she watched lines of experienced western dancers kick up their heels.

Brett grabbed her hand and pulled her up. "C'mon, our food's settled and there's an open spot right down there," he said, pointing to where one dancing couple had just retired, but Lauren froze.

"I can't do *that*," she objected. "I can barely slow dance. I don't know any of those steps they're doing. I'd have to learn first."

"Best way to learn is doing."

"Brett." She shook her head, tugging at his hand, but he yanked her up against him and gazed down into her face.

"I want you to dance with me, Lauren," he murmured as he lowered his head and kissed her right there in the middle of the crowd. It wasn't a polite, public kiss, either. Anyone watching would know the passion that existed between them, and she found herself moving up closer, seeking his heat, her sense of daring kicking in. Hell, any excuse to be this close to Brett was a good one. What did she care if she made a fool of herself?

"Okay," she whispered.

"Just watch me, and the person in front of you. Don't try the more complicated steps at first, but you'll pick it up faster than you think," he reassured, leading her forward to the vacant spot.

It was hard for the first few minutes, but as he showed her the steps a little more slowly than the crowd was dancing, she caught the rhythm, and nearly waved her hat in the air she was so excited to actually be doing it.

Breathless and having the most fun she probably ever had in years, she fell against him as the music changed from a stomping beat to something slow and sexy. Some of the dancers left the floor for a drink, while others moved closer to each other as the lights around them dimmed.

"You did great, not that I had any doubts," he whispered. For all the exertion, he wasn't even winded. "Your body knows how to move. Seen it here, seen it on horseback, seen it in bed," he said seductively, and she pressed her pelvis against him, cradling the hardness that he pressed back.

The world dwindled away, and it was just the two of them, moving to the music. Brett wrapped her hand in his, bringing it up to his lips as they danced. She held on a little tighter, feeling a shudder work down to her toes.

"Maybe it's time to go home," he said against her mouth. "Unless you want to stay and dance some more."

She wanted to dance, she thought with a mischievous smile, but maybe she'd really let loose and try it back at the ranch, and tempt Brett with a little western-style striptease.

"Going home sounds good. Let me just go to the ladies' room first. You know where it is?"

He pointed to a hallway at the back past the bar, and she wound through the crowd. As she neared the hallway, she found a line that discouraged her goal—it would probably take as long to drive back to the ranch as it would to wait. Turning to make her way back to the crowd, she passed the vestibule

where coats were hung, and heard familiar voices—
Pete and Graciela.

Not meaning to eavesdrop, she couldn't help it
once she caught a snippet of conversation that held
her in place.

"I told you it was a bad idea to get involved with
these people, Gracie. Why couldn't you just marry
me and we would have figured it out?"

Pete's voice was urgent, upset, and Graciela
spoke quickly and in Spanish, which clearly Pete
understood, but Lauren did not.

"They're dangerous, baby. We could have found
another way to bring your parents here. We shouldn't
have done this." Lauren heard the pause, the girl's
response, still in Spanish, and clearly miserable and
frightened.

"How much more do you need?"

She answered, and Lauren heard Pete curse. Lauren didn't know the details, but it sounded as if Pete
was caught up with some scheme to get Graciela's
parents over the border. Maybe she'd been wrong
about Pete. It appeared as if he'd gotten himself in
over his head with the wrong girl. Brett needed to
know. Lauren was certain of that.

Making her way through the crowd with a sense
of urgency, she didn't see Brett, and asked one of the
hands she recognized from the ranch. She didn't
know his name, and the assessing look in his eye
bothered her as he gestured toward the door without

saying a word. Apparently, Brett was out by the truck, though she found it odd that he hadn't waited for her.

As she went out into the dusty parking lot, she saw Brett near the truck—with a woman. They were arguing. Several groups of smokers had gathered around the lot, and they were listening with interest. She wondered who the woman was, and what was going on. She couldn't just stand here by herself. She was with Brett, and she had every right to join him now, argument or no argument. Maybe she could even help.

"Brett?" she interrupted questioningly, looking first at the woman, and then at him. "Is everything all right?" Lauren asked as she observed the anger in his eyes.

He wiped a hand over his face, and she felt the tension emanating off of him. Something was definitely wrong. She wanted to reach out, to comfort, but he'd withdrawn big time. She waited for him to say something.

"Lauren, I'm sorry, I need a moment, please. Can you go back in, find Pete, hang with him for a few minutes? I'll be back shortly." His voice was strained and Lauren's attention turned toward the sound of a slamming door.

Lauren would have gladly given Brett some privacy and escaped the tension, but the woman stepped forward, her hard blue gaze pinning Lauren in place.

"What? You don't want your girlfriend finding out about me? I'd say the cat's out of the bag, darlin'." She laughed, though it cut through the air around them like a whip.

Brett stepped forward, his body rigid, the look in his eye more dangerous than Lauren had ever seen.

"Marsha, this isn't the time or the place."

"You. Who are you?" the woman asked her point-blank. Lauren paused and faced her, not intimidated—she didn't even know this woman let alone feel intimidated by her.

"That would be none of your business, actually," Lauren answered just as coldly.

"It is if you've been screwing my *fiancé's* brains out, but don't get too excited, honey, you're just the flavor of the month."

Lauren was speechless, the emotional wind knocked out of her. A few other shadowy figures in the lot and by the doors appeared around the edges of her vision, onlookers keeping their distance, but no doubt hearing the confrontation. This Marsha person wasn't bothered with keeping her voice down. All Lauren could do was repeat the word weakly,

"Fiancé?"

She looked at Brett questioningly, but he didn't meet her gaze. She automatically glanced at the left hand of the woman in front of them, noticing a large, sparkling diamond on her ring finger. Lauren felt the bottom drop out of her stomach and thought she might be sick.

She looked at Brett again, and repeated, "Fiancé?"

He met her eyes, his jaw tight. "*Ex*-fiancé."

Lauren didn't know what to think, the other woman jumping in between them so quickly that she didn't have any time to respond.

"You left me at the altar, Brett. Two weeks ago today you left me to face all of those people, alone." The beautiful blonde's voice choked, and she seemed to shrink back a little as Brett, fierce and furious, looked around them and hissed a response between clenched teeth.

Lauren barely heard him warn the woman not to air their laundry in public. The conversation fell to the background as she processed the fact that Brett had been running away from his own wedding—his wedding to *this* woman—when she'd found him at the side of the road.

His wedding, the phrase reverberated in her mind, every other thought banished.

Lauren looked up at the tall, statuesque blonde— she was supermodel gorgeous, if a little hard around the eyes. She was supposed to have been Brett's wife. Though he'd said *ex*-fiancé, but the storming woman between them obviously didn't agree. And it had only been two weeks.

If Brett was engaged to this woman, to Marsha, what did that make Lauren? The other woman?

She lifted her gaze to meet the woman's self-satisfied smirk and felt ill again, needing to escape. Life was showing Lauren once more that her impulsive decisions would come back and stomp on her every time. Especially the decisions she made about men.

How could she have been so stupid? At least if she'd listened to Becky, and if she'd left after that first night, she would have had the memory of a great night with a great guy, and she would have been able to hold on to that.

Now all she had was the poisoned feeling of being a fool ten times over. Needing to escape the intense curiosity of all the people watching them, she ran back to the bar, feeling trapped, but needing to find some place she could hide out, if just for the moment.

As she staggered through the throng of bodies, she couldn't stop the tears from coming, and felt a strong hand grab her wrist.

"Hey, darlin'. What are those tears for? Your man go and leave you behind?" A cowboy she didn't recognize slid up a little too close, winding his arm around her waist before she could say anything, and she just shook her head, pushing him away. He'd obviously had too much to drink and didn't realize she wasn't interested.

"No. thank you, I don't want to dance," she said, pushing away harder, but he just hauled her up closer.

"That's a different little accent you have there—stranger in town? And a pretty one, too," he said with a leer. His hand held her wrist too tightly, and as she pulled away, it hurt.

"You're hurting me—let go!" she finally shouted above the din and kicked him with the pointy toe of her boot directly in the shin. A chorus of questioning voices broke out around them as a few other men stepped forward, and Lauren backed up, unsure if they were going to defend her or their friend. She rubbed her wrist, and was so relieved when Pete stepped up by her that her knees almost gave out.

"You okay? What's going on? Where's Brett?"

Lauren looked at him and just shook her head, tears flooding again as he quickly slipped his arm around her shoulders and led her away from the crowd.

9

BRETT HAD NEVER BEEN SO FURIOUS in his life, and was angered even more so by having this showdown in front of people he knew and worked with.

"You want to say anything else to me, Marsha, we'll do it tomorrow in private," Brett stated flatly, turning for the bar to go find Lauren. She'd been devastated, and he was kicking himself. He had to find a way to fix it.

"Oh, *now* you want privacy, after you very publicly left me standing at the front of the church, abandoned, having to explain that you weren't showing up?" she accused, loudly, even daring to sniff pitifully. Sherry had shown up at her side; apparently, they'd come together for girls' night out, and his manager was glaring at him with contempt.

Marsha's posturing as a victim made him disgusted and angrier than he'd been in a long time. He'd kept the truth between himself and Pete because he'd been too upset and embarrassed about what had really happened at the wedding.

He'd rather no one ever know that his wife-to-be

had not only been doing his best man before the service, but then had run off with the guy on the honeymoon. All anyone knew as that Brett had taken off, and the wedding hadn't happened. Why did everyone need to know the truth?

Then he'd met Lauren, and he felt his chest squeeze, now hit by the enormity of his mistake. He'd been so caught up in placating his own wounded ego that he hadn't thought about the repercussions for Lauren.

In all truth, he'd never imagined they'd have more than a fling, or that what happened at the wedding would ever matter as much as it was mattering now.

Not even Marsha knew that he knew—that he'd witnessed what she'd done, up close. Because of that her days of playing him were over. He faced her, aware of Sherry's glare and not caring—maybe it was time everyone knew the truth, and he'd just have to deal with it.

"I don't know what game you're playing, or what you want," he said under his breath, and then he was hit with a spark of realization. "Howie dumped you, didn't he? And now you're crawling back to me, and trying to make *me* out to be the bad guy. I guess you figured I really did take off that day, cold feet or something, but that's not exactly right. Do you really think I'm that stupid? I could have warned you about Howie—he never stays with one woman for very long."

To her credit, Marsha froze, paling slightly under her tan. "I don't know what you're accusing me of—"

Brett didn't bother lowering his voice, either.

"Do you want me to describe in detail what I saw you doing in the dressing room with Howie about a half-hour before the ceremony? Right before I supposedly *abandoned* you? I'd be happy to let everyone know, since you apparently don't want to discuss this in private," he added with a sarcastic drawl, though his gut was roiling. He could see the shock on her face, and Sherry's, and got some small satisfaction from that.

Sherry's arms dropped from where she'd had them crossed over her chest.

"What *did* you do with Howie, Marsha?" Sherry asked, sounding apprehensive.

So Sherry hadn't known; that provided Brett with some degree of relief. At least his staff hadn't been laughing at him behind his back the whole time for being duped by his best man and his bride-to-be.

Marsha stuttered, looking for something to say, her eyes welling with "I've been caught red-handed" tears. Brett didn't feel an iota of sympathy.

"It was a weak moment," she said in a much lower tone of voice, looking from side to side. She needn't worry—the only ones close enough to hear were he and Sherry, though he was sure word would get around soon enough.

"You mean to say that was the first time you'd had sex with Howie? Never mind," he said, holding up a hand to stem her comment. "I don't want to know, and it doesn't matter. You two took off on our honeymoon, though you let everyone think you went alone? The poor, abandoned bride? Give up the victim act, Marsha. And give the ring back as well. It was my mother's after all," he said, hating that she'd ever worn it.

Sherry stepped back. "Oh, Marsha, how could you? You lied to everyone, even me! If you and Brett were having problems, we could have talked about it."

Brett frowned at the thought of Marsha and Sherry discussing their relationship, but then again, he was relieved that Sherry was hearing the truth. Maybe she'd let up on Lauren from now on—if there was finally a from now on. Marsha's tears dried up as if by magic, and she practically spit, taking the ring off.

"*Fine*. Though I wouldn't stand there all self-righteous if I were you. You didn't exactly waste time replacing me, from what Sherry says."

Marsha threw the ring at him, and he caught it before it fell into the dirt. The careless gesture with his family heirloom was the final straw. Stepping forward to face her up close, he made his feelings crystal clear.

"It's over, Marsha. We probably never should have been together in the first place, but everyone makes mistakes. I'm willing to accept that I probably made a few as well, which is why all this happened. So for that, I'm sorry. But if I hear word of you speaking anything but the truth about this, you'll regret it. I promise you that. You can tell Howie the same," he snapped.

"I won't be seeing Howie anymore."

"Big surprise. Maybe he'll come back around. You really do deserve each other, I think."

Seething as she spun away, Marsha stomped to the car and slammed the door, obviously waiting for Sherry to join her.

"I'm sorry, Brett, really I thought the worst of you," Sherry said softly, still looking shocked and ashamed. "But why didn't you let anyone know?"

Brett shook his head. He couldn't deal with this now, explaining to Sherry why he'd done what he did. He knew he owed Lauren an explanation, though. At least that much.

"Brett?"

"I just couldn't, Sherry. I just couldn't tell everyone," he said, looking to the bar instead of at Sherry.

"I guess I can see that."

"Don't you have to go?"

Sherry laughed. "Her car. The bitch can drive herself. I can call Paul for a ride, or catch someone here."

"Okay."

"You here with Lauren?"

He nodded.

"I take it she knows."

"Not all of it."

"Then maybe you should go clear the air."

He nodded again and took a deep breath. "You sure you're okay to get a ride home?"

"Absolutely. Go."

Brett walked quickly to the bar, and searched over the sea of hats looking for Lauren's but he couldn't find her.

"You looking for that chick you were dancing with?"

He nodded to the woman he recognized from the line dance earlier. "Yeah."

"Sorry, cowboy, but she had a little scuffle here and left with some other guy, a young stud. Cute as hell, too."

Shit, he cursed silently, stalking back out the door, his brain frying at the thought of Lauren out there with some strange guy who picked her up in the bar. She'd been upset, vulnerable, and not all cowboys were gentlemen, far from it.

He had to find a way to make her listen, to make her believe he wasn't the louse she must be thinking he was. He had to find a way to convince her to stay. But first he had to find her and make sure she was all right.

"PETE, TAKE ME BACK to the ranch," Lauren demanded. He hung back though, his hands in his pockets.

"You should go back with Brett, and I'm here, uh, with—"

"Graciela, we know."

"We?"

"Brett knows. He saw you two kissing in the corner."

Pete rubbed a hand over his face. "Great. What did he say?"

Lauren stared at him. "I don't really want to talk about that right now."

"You two have a fight?"

"No, he's with his fiancée at the moment," she said her voice trembling.

"Ah, no, Lauren. Marsha? Marsha was here, too?"

"That's her—tall blonde, engaged to your brother who apparently ditched her at the altar and then brought me home, then yeah, that's her. Can we go now?"

"Brett will worry where you got to."

"I doubt it," she said peevishly, miserable.

"Lauren, he's not with her—it's not what you think."

"He wasn't engaged to her two weeks ago, about to be married?"

"Well, yeah, but—"

"No buts, that's pretty much the story she told, and it's all I need to know. Can you drive me back, please? I want to pack and be out of here first thing in the morning." She set her hand on her hip for emphasis, and winced.

"You all right?"

"Yeah. I think that guy bruised my fingers, or I sprained it or something."

Pete's expression clouded over and he stepped forward, taking her hand. "I should go back in there and beat the crap out of him."

"He was just drunk."

"No excuse. He'll know better than to get that drunk the next time."

She smiled, thinking how much he was like his older brother, and felt tears start to build again. Pete's eyes went wide with panic.

"Okay, listen, don't cry. We'll get it all straightened out. I'll drive you home, but we'll go out front to tell Brett first. He will worry," Pete said.

Lauren shrugged. Pete went in to tell Graciela he'd be back within the hour, and when he returned she was already sitting in his truck. As they drove around the corner of the building into the front lot, they noticed Brett's truck was already gone.

"Damn."

"Guess he had better things to do," Lauren said hollowly. "Are you sure you should leave Graciela back there? Is it safe?"

"Safe? Sure—she knows most of the people in the place."

"I don't mean that, I—I," Lauren took a deep

breath, and just came out with it. "I heard you talking earlier. I didn't mean to, but I heard you say she'd gotten herself into something dangerous."

Pete turned to her, his features strained. "She won't marry me without bringing her parents to the states first. Her father is ill and not getting the medical attention he needs in Mexico, and she's been sending him money. Or I thought that's what she was doing. Turns out, she also got involved with some bad people running an illegal smuggling operation."

"Drugs?" Lauren asked, shocked.

"No, at least not that I know of. They smuggle people."

"Bringing illegal aliens over the border," she said, remembering what Brett had said.

"Yes, it's not only against the law but deadly dangerous, even more so these days. But once she made a deal with them, they're not the kind of men who let you just change your mind. They also threatened to hurt her family if she didn't come up with the whole amount to bring her parents over."

"How much?"

"Ten-thousand dollars, U.S. Five thousand each," Pete declared, his lips formed in a tense, straight line.

"Oh, Pete. This is bad. Why can't she just go to the authorities—the Border Patrol—and report them?" She forgot about her problems for a moment, focusing on him and Graciela.

"She's here illegally herself, Lauren, and now she's tied into these guys. The authorities could arrest her for more than being without papers."

"That doesn't make it right, Pete."

"I know, but I love her. I hate seeing her suffer like this. I know how scared she is, and for her parents, too. These smugglers, you have no idea how they victimize these people at the same time they promise them everything. Sometimes they take the money and never even make good on their promises, or the people die in transit, or get arrested and sent back, sometimes having sold everything to pay the smugglers."

"Why didn't you go to Brett? There must have been ways to make this work."

"Are you kidding? Brett would have a fit if he knew, and he'd probably ship Graciela back to Mexico."

Lauren drew back, defending Brett even though he'd broken her heart. "That's not fair. You never even gave him a chance." She covered her face with her hands.

"Take it from me, he wouldn't understand."

Lauren took a deep breath, unsure. Maybe Pete was right. Did she really know Brett at all? In the end, this was a family issue, and at this point, it was better left that way. She'd be gone in the morning, and they would all just figure it out without her.

LAUREN ACHED ALL OVER, physically and emotionally. Pete had dropped her at the ranch house, and luckily Brett wasn't home—off mending fences with his former lover, no doubt.

The hot shower had helped some, but she couldn't sleep, and so she packed her few things to leave in the morning.

She was wearing only her terry robe when someone knocked on her door. She opened it slowly, expecting Brett. To her surprise, and disappointment, she found Sherry, holding a dinner tray.

"Sherry," Lauren said, not knowing what to say to her.

"I know you had a bad night. I thought you might like a little Mexican hot chocolate to help," Sherry said contritely, with what seemed like concern for her welfare. She deposited the tray on a nearby table.

"You didn't need to do that," Lauren fibbed, though the scent of the spicy chocolate made her stomach gurgle. She yanked her robe a little more snugly around her. "Thank you. What do you mean, I had a bad night?" She suddenly got what Sherry had said.

Sherry walked back to the door and put her hand on the knob, then paused there, looking down, and then at Lauren. Lauren waited for what Sherry obviously had come to say, though she couldn't imagine what it was.

Sherry took a deep breath. "I was with Marsha at the bar earlier, and I heard her and Brett arguing. I wanted to say I'm sorry for offering you such a cold welcome to the ranch. You see, I'd befriended Marsha when she was seeing Brett, and we'd developed some kind of closeness over that time, and I figured, well," she drifted off. "I thought, when Brett brought you home, on the heels of standing her up at the altar, it seemed like…"

"Don't worry. I can guess what it seemed like to everyone," Lauren managed, feeling the same wash of embarrassment she'd been through earlier.

"I'm sorry for that, too—because no one had any place to think that way, including me. It was very unfair, to you and to Brett."

Lauren found herself warming to Sherry. "You were just protecting your friend. That's not a bad thing," she said, remembering how Becky always stood up for her.

"Yeah, a friend who was screwing around on Brett, which I guess I should have known. I knew Marsha was the kind of woman to seek male attention and a lot of it, but I thought it would be different with Brett. I was wrong."

Lauren sat down on the edge of the bed, wondering what Sherry was really getting at. "She was cheating on him?"

"I thought you already knew that. Brett said you were there."

Lauren shook her head. "I left with Pete. I haven't seen Brett. His truck was gone, and I figured he went off with Marsha."

Sherry shook her head, saying something under her breath in Spanish. "No, Marsha left in her own car, that I know."

"Maybe he went after her."

Sherry looked baffled. "No, something else happened."

Just at that moment, they heard the rumbling of an engine outside Lauren's window. "That's probably him right now. I've already said more than I should, but I wanted to say I was sorry for my own part in this. For the rest, you should talk to Brett, but," she smiled somewhat hopefully before continuing, "when this is all cleared up, I hope we can be friends."

Lauren grimaced, unsure how she felt about anything, including having Sherry acting like her new best friend.

"Thanks, but I'm not sure I'll be around past morning."

Sherry grinned in a secretive, knowing way. "If you're smart, you will be. Brett's one in a million."

"That may be—" Lauren started to say before Sherry interrupted again,

"Give him a chance. He may not have made the best decisions, but he wasn't acting maliciously. I can guarantee you that. It's hard for a man when he takes a blow like Brett did. It makes them feel like less than a whole man, and he wasn't thinking straight."

Before Lauren could ask what she meant, Sherry was gone.

10

BRETT WAS HALF-CRAZY when he got home, but he'd checked everywhere he could, scouring every place he could think of to find Lauren, until his eyes started blurring from exhaustion and he had to give in and come home. He had no claim on her—she was a grown woman, and if she'd left with another guy, that was her right. Yet it felt like someone was tearing his heart out to even think that. If something had happened to her…

"She's upstairs. Pete brought her home. You didn't know?" Sherry asked, meeting up with him on the staircase.

He felt a wave of relief at Sherry's words. "Why are you here so late?"

"Just had a feeling I should be."

"She's here? Safe?"

"Both. And heartbroken. You can fix that." Sherry crossed her arms, staring down at him from the top step.

"If she'll let me."

"Just go. I'll use one of the guest rooms tonight. See you in the morning."

Brett nodded and raced up the stairs. He knocked softly, and the door opened. At least he'd gotten that far.

"You are here—thank God. I looked everywhere," he said in a rush of words.

"I came home with Pete. We looked for you, and you were already gone. I figured you left with... her," she added stiffly.

"No way in hell. I guess we must have circled around each other, and I heard you took off with some guy. Never even thought of Pete." He smiled, but she didn't smile back. "I was scared to death that you were out there with some stranger."

She cocked an eyebrow at him. "Guess that makes sense since it's how I ran into you."

"Lauren, I didn't mean it like that."

"Whatever. Sorry you worried."

He caught sight of her bags stacked in the corner. "Going somewhere?"

"Did you really expect me to stay?"

"I expected us to...talk."

"Fine, talk," she said angrily, and picked up the cup of cocoa, not thinking, dropping it as she couldn't support the weight with her sore hand.

"What happened?" he demanded, lifting her hand. "You hurt yourself. There's swelling—"

"I had a little altercation with a drunken cowboy when I went back in the bar. Mostly harmless, but he grabbed my wrist and I tried to pull away and hurt myself."

"Who was it?"

"I don't know. How would I know? Pete stepped in. I'm fine. It's just a little sore," she said tiredly.

"I hate that you got hurt, and that I wasn't there to help."

"You obviously had more important things to do," she said peevishly and hated herself for showing that side of her emotions, but the truth was she was jealous, humiliated, and her heart ached far more than her wrist.

He gently inspected her hand again. "Well, I'm no doctor, and we can get an X-ray tomorrow, but I think it's just badly bruised. I'll get you an ice pack."

"Don't bother. I really just want to go to bed. I have to make an early start."

"I don't want you to go," he said baldly. When she didn't look at him for a few long minutes, he thought his chest would explode.

"Sherry said something about Marsha cheating on you. Is that true?"

"Yes, though I wish Sherry wouldn't gossip about my business."

"She thought I already knew, and if it helps, she put in a good word for you."

"Did it work?"

"I'm talking to you, aren't I?"

"Right."

She sat down on the side of the bed, looking as exhausted as she said she was, and defeated. He hated himself for that.

"So was I your revenge, Brett? Your retaliation, to make Marsha jealous? I guess it worked," she said, sighing.

He looked at her like she had lost her mind. "Retaliation? You think what's between you and me was *retaliation*? You thought I was using you all that time? Lauren." He swallowed hard, shaking his head, and then met her eyes. "I guess that might be true on some level, but not in the way you think. I wasn't trying to make Marsha jealous. I could care less if I ever saw her again."

"C'mon, Brett, you were going to be married to her less than two weeks ago! You have to be in denial."

"I'm a grown man, Lauren, I know my emotions. Just because I don't talk about them a lot doesn't mean I'm in denial. Let me start at the beginning, okay, so we don't just end up going in circles?"

She nodded wearily, and he sat down in the chair across from her, their knees almost touching. As she listened, he made himself tell her everything— no matter how humiliating it was, how private, he shared it all.

When he was done, he felt emptied out, but hopeful. "That's about it. It's not a complicated story. I never asked her to marry me. It was one of those things that just sort of happens, and I never stopped it because I didn't think I would find anything better, to be honest. Marriage and romance haven't been high on my list of priorities, and Marsha didn't seem to mind me spending all my time on the ranch. Of course, now that I know she was fooling around with Howie, I realize that she was probably unhappy as well. I was going to the church to break it off, and when I caught them going at it, I didn't know how to handle it, so I took off."

She nodded. "I guess I might have done the same."

"Running away from your problems is never a good choice. I didn't think I'd see her again, let alone like that, and I guess when Howie dumped her, she couldn't take it, and figured I'd take her back, not knowing I knew the truth. I have no idea. It's all so screwed up," he said, sighing in disgust.

Lauren processed what he'd told her. "So, you caught them having sex and left. I get that. That's why you were driving your motorcycle down the road like a madman that day? You were angry?"

"I wasn't driving like a— okay, yeah, I was pissed left, right, sideways. I felt like the biggest kind of fool."

"I can relate," she added, watching him wince for a quick second before he went on.

"The thing is, I realized I was angry, but I wasn't hurt. Not in the broken-hearted way you'd expect. My ego took a dent—no man likes to think the woman he's with has cheated on him, but I was almost…relieved. Like I'd gotten a second chance. I think that's why I left instead of beating the crap out of Howie."

"And then you met me."

He smiled in a slanted, sexy way that she'd already come to love.

"Yeah. Then I met you."

"You said, when I asked if you'd used me to make her jealous, that I wasn't that far from the truth. What did you mean?"

Brett stood, shoving his hands deep into his jeans pockets and walked to the window. He didn't say anything for several, long minutes, so she just waited.

"This is difficult. I didn't use you—not in any purposeful, conscious way. But I guess when you came to the door that night, and we had such spectacular sex, I didn't want to let·you go because… shit." He closed his eyes, his head dropping back before he stood straight again, and looked her in the eye. "I suppose it was that you were my second chance. Not retribution, but maybe…redemption, or affirmation, or something like that. Dammit, I don't know."

She sat back, befuddled. "I don't get it—redemption for what? What did you do wrong?"

He blew out a breath. "Lauren, when I saw them together that morning, what I saw between them was so raw, and so passionate, that I knew I'd failed somewhere along the way. As a man. Sex had never been like that for me and Marsha."

"There are a lot of reasons people cheat, Brett. Sometimes it could be because they're not happy, but you're a wonderful lover," she said. "Believe me, I've been with a man who didn't care about his partner. Even then, that's no reason for someone to go outside the relationship, let alone on their wedding day. She was wrong, and that's not because of you. You can't blame yourself for her choices. There's no way she can make you less of a man."

"Well, I figure it always takes two."

"That may be true, but don't take more responsibility than is yours. Lots of couples may not have mind-blowing sex, but if they care about each other, they figure it out. You and Marsha were obviously wrong from the beginning. It wasn't the sex. The sex was just a symptom of everything else being wrong."

He nodded quietly. "Thanks."

She felt the heat spread up from her toes when he looked at her in just that way. Suddenly, she was painfully aware that she was naked beneath the robe.

"I just don't know what to think, Brett. I understand your side of it a little better now, but that doesn't make it less humiliating. Why didn't you tell me? Or tell someone? Do you know how everyone reacted when you brought me here? Do you realize what they must have thought?"

"I do—now. I guess at the time I thought I could

avoid it all. I wanted to keep my personal business private, and I never counted on meeting anyone, let alone dragging you into the middle of it."

"Okay," she said, nodding slowly, some of the hurt relenting. "I can accept that."

"I thought what we had was…you know, short-term. But I don't want it to end. I wanted us to have a magical night tonight, Lauren, and I planned to tell you everything and to ask you to stay—then it all blew up in my face. But it hurt you the most. I don't know what I can do to make up for that, but I want the chance to try."

"Brett, I don't want you thinking you have to make things up. I don't need that. After Wes, I had no idea what to expect from being with a man— you've made me so…" She paused, the color infusing her cheeks. "You made me feel so female, so sexy… with you, it's like I can do anything. I guess that's why it killed me to think it was all a sham."

His gaze was so sincere she trembled when she took in the sheer emotion there. He was being completely open with her and she couldn't look away.

"Nothing between us was ever that, Lauren. Not from the first time I touched you."

Her hand throbbed less, and lightness infused her soul.

"Brett, I want so much to believe this," she whispered, her need ragged in her voice, along with her lingering confusion.

He walked up to her, standing closer, framing her face in his hands. "You can believe it. I'll never lie to you again, never give you less than one hundred percent of me. I promise. I'll never hurt you again, Lauren, if you'll stay so that we can see what we have, because I think it's something incredible." His hands slipped down her shoulders to her arms, and he lifted her bruised fingers to his lips, kissing them lightly.

"I'm sorry I wasn't there when this happened. But I'll make sure it never happens ever again, if you give me the chance"

"Oh Brett." Her breath caught, knowing he meant every word, but also knowing he shouldn't put such expectations on himself or their budding relationship. *Relationship.* The word sent a shiver down her spine. Not a fling or a one-night stand or whatever else they'd thought they had. Something much, much more.

"You can't insulate me from everything, and I don't want you to. I've been there, done that. I didn't like it. I don't want you to shield me from life, but it might be nice if we can try sharing it for a while, and seeing what happens," she agreed softly.

"Fair enough. We have a lot to learn about each other, I guess," he whispered, pushing her hair back and running his lips along the curve of her ear, which made her spin.

"We have time. I'm not going anywhere," she answered, her heart pounding.

His hands settled lightly on her waist, as if he were afraid to touch her too firmly, intent on not hurting her or scaring her away. Her head dropped back, exposing her throat to his kisses, stoking the need for more.

Though they were both being careful, she knew that in the last few hours they'd crossed a line they'd both been dancing around for days. There was nothing tentative about what she wanted from Brett, and she didn't want him afraid to touch her, treating her with kid gloves. She'd had enough of that all of her life. He'd hurt her, but he'd been hurt as well; they'd worked through it, and now they needed to move on.

Yanking the tie at her waist, she let her robe fall open and shrugged it from her shoulders. Wrapping her bare arms around his neck, she pushed up on her toes so that she was pressed against him, capturing his lips in a kiss that was anything but tentative. He murmured his approval and with his help she hitched herself up, wrapping her legs around his hips and showing him in no uncertain terms how he made her feel, and what he made her want.

She caught her breath a little, however, when his fingers cupped her backside, supporting her. She'd forgotten the bruise she had from riding the day before—it had been the first time she'd fallen off her horse. And she'd climbed right back on, and that was the kind of woman she wanted to be.

He broke the kiss, lowering her, his breathing

ragged as they both looked down to where his hand had been and found a large purple and green bruise forming.

"Oh, God, honey, I'm so sorry," he murmured.

"It's a bruise, Brett. I'll live. I imagine I'll get them from time to time if I keep riding horses." She smiled wryly, taking his hand and moving it to her breast as she wiggled up closer to him again. "Now where were we?"

"Maybe you should rest for now. It's been a long night, it's late," he suggested gently, though his hand didn't move and he massaged the area lightly. It gave her an idea.

"A soak in your tub and a massage would be wonderful," she said innocently, though there was nothing chaste about the way she arched into his touch.

"That's not a bad idea. Why don't you go down to my room, and I'll meet you there."

"Where are you going?"

"I'm hungry, now that the knots in my stomach are gone. I'll get some wine and a snack." He touched her face, and the tenderness in his expression nearly did her in. "Don't worry. I won't be long. You go relax. Let me take care of you."

She could see it was important to him and relented; she supposed they would learn how to take care of each other.

"Okay. I guess I can go along with that."

"Good, now scoot."

He smiled, picking up her robe from the floor, and she slipped it on, kissing him outside of the door. She was giddy. Could this really be happening? Could it be as good as she thought? As she walked down to his room, excitement and anticipation moved her feet along a little faster. She was looking forward to the long, hot soak anyway, especially since she'd be sharing it with the man of her dreams.

BRETT STARED DOWN at Lauren as she slept, smiling to himself. It was pre-dawn, still dark except for a silvery light that came in from the window, and the house was quiet. An habitual early riser, he always liked this time of day, before things got crazy, though he couldn't imagine anything crazier than the day before.

A tray with wineglasses and some snacks sat, the food untouched, on a table across the room. When he'd returned from the kitchen, Lauren had been asleep on his side of the bed. It was fine; they had time, he thought with renewed happiness. Everything was out in the open, and he was glad for it.

He smiled when she raised her hand and touched his face.

"You're awake."

"Mmm-hmm. Hard to break the early riser thing even when I've only been asleep for a few hours."

She snuggled against him underneath the warm blankets, her skin hot and soft, and he turned hard.

She stretched and groaned again. "I guess I never made it to the hot tub last night. Sorry about that. Last thing I remember is hitting this bed."

"Yeah, you pretty much passed out, which is fine. You needed the sleep. Come here." He gathered her gently against him, "Why don't you snooze some more?"

The friction of her body moving against his was setting him on fire. Still, he figured they could both use the rest. She apparently had different ideas, and he jumped when her hand curled around his erection.

"Hey," he said, his voice husky, startled.

"Hey back." She yawned again, and smiled at him. "I figured since we're both awake…"

He disengaged her fingers from his erection, reluctantly, but with the patience of a man who was counting on better things to come.

"Wait here," he whispered, and walked to the bathroom, returning a few minutes later with a spicy smelling organic liniment he'd gotten from a guest who'd practiced homeopathic medicine. It was apparently edible, and though he'd had his doubts, it also worked. It would have to serve a more erotic purpose at the moment.

Drawing the covers down, he sat on the end of the bed.

"Flip over. Relax," he commanded softly, and saw her pause, looking at him through the soft gray shadows of the room before doing as he asked. He could see the silhouette of her body against the stark white sheets as a little more light crept in. The image took his breath away, as if she weren't quite real.

He slid over, carefully swinging his knee over the backs of her thighs and straddling her in a way that was both achingly erotic and practical. Trying to ignore the sensual shocks his cock endured as the tip brushed against the curve of her ass every time he leaned in, he warmed the lotion in his hands and worked from her shoulders down. He closed his eyes, his pulse hammering as she moaned in pleasure.

"Just tell me what you like," he managed, his voice choked in his throat. If she moaned again, he might just lose it.

"Brett, this is fantastic…oh…there," she sighed as he kneaded her lower back.

He wanted her, there was no doubt about that, but he was also enjoying just making her feel good. That she responded to him so easily, with so much trust, especially in view of what had happened, humbled him.

"This liniment has some warmth to it, which is good for your bruised bum, too. But it won't burn, so I'm going to try to rub some over your hip, okay? Let me know if I'm too rough."

"Okay." She sounded slumberous and sexy, making it difficult to keep his focus, brushing his fingers over the curve where the dark bruise was becoming more prominent, and rubbing a little more when she didn't protest.

He took in the tender spot, the discoloration. She was right, all riders fell and got bruised up from time to time, but something about the injury made him feel fiercely protective. It was apparently an emotion Lauren brought out in the people around her, for better or worse. Still, he understood her need to stand on her own two feet, and respected it. The West was home to strong men and strong women, and Lauren was going to fit in just fine.

Satisfied that he'd worked enough lotion in, he took his time with her legs. She had shapely, strong legs. He'd never given a massage like this, and found it was a slow exploration that he was relishing.

He caressed each cord of muscle reaching down the back of her thighs, moving his hands along her skin from foot to hip, then slowing down and threading his fingertips along the hollows at the back of her knee.

She quivered, and he noted how in certain spots she responded more than others, and returned to those for a second time. He trailed the touch along the inside of her thigh until she sighed, opening her legs a little, obviously wanting him to make his massage a little more intimate.

He was happy to oblige, her moans becoming a little louder as he eased his fingers along the warm, silky-slick crevice of her sex, finding her clit. She was swollen and hot, and he intended to make her hotter.

"The lotion, it's…warm there, too," she gasped.

"Is that okay?"

"Oh yes…much better than okay," she purred, lifting her hips to rock against him. He leaned over to nip the soft skin of her ass on the side that wasn't bruised as he massaged the hot flesh that swelled against his fingers. Twisting his hand just so, he slid first one finger inside of her, then two, until she was lifting up to support herself on her elbows, pushing back, riding his hand.

He met her rhythm, knowing what she liked, when to speed up, when to slow down, and when she was so close to the edge that he could feel the tightness around his fingers ready to let loose, he withdrew. She cried out in objection, twisting to face him.

"Brett! Please!" The plea came out on a moan, and he angled up behind her, hanging on the jagged edge himself.

"Don't worry, sweetheart. I'm right here."

He made sure he took care with her injured hip and nudged the crease where his fingers had been with his cock. Her hot skin tempted him, and he tortured them both for a few incredible minutes, sliding back and forth. "You were having so much fun you convinced me to join you," he teased, finding her opening and easing inside with tight satisfaction that nearly made him come far too quickly.

Taking deep breaths, he fought for control, reciting a litany of unsexy thoughts in his head until his body backed away from the edge of arousal he was teetering on. Lauren lifted up, grabbing the sturdy support of his headboard with her hands, pushing back and tearing that control to shreds. The sight of her before him, posed like some sex goddess, taking him so deep and hard pushed him back to the edge, and his excitement burst from him in a stream of sexy encouragement that let her know everything he was seeing, liking, feeling.

Had he ever felt this good with anyone? Her body stretched and formed around him and he moved inside, buried so deep that the soft pubic hair of her mound brushed his balls. Reaching up to torture them both just a little more, he closed his hands around her breasts and pinched her erect nipples, making her buck against him hard.

"Careful, sweetheart, I'm too close," he managed on a ragged breath.

"Good. I want you to lose it, Brett. I want you to give me everything. I need *you to give me everything*," she urged, setting a rhythm that dared him to do anything but. She moaned out his name, clenching and hugging him inside her body as she came again.

Brett let go, thrusting hard into his own climax, their skin slapping together hard as his body moved of its own volition.

"Oh, God, Brett, yes," she cried, spasms of pleasure rippling through her body. Even more excited by watching her, hearing her, he held her hips firmly in his hands. Amazingly, even after coming once, he was hard and wanted more. Continuing to stroke deeply, keeping up the rhythm, he catapulted them both through one more orgasm, their joining a wet, hot slick of spent passion.

As he backed away from her, he stood at the side of the bed, his knees actually feeling weak. The idea made him chuckle to himself. Somehow the idea of Lauren making him a little weak in the knees was okay—more than okay—not that he was going to be announcing that to anyone.

"I guess it's true what they say about make up sex," she said on a husky note, looking at him from the bed, posed in the first rays of morning sunlight. She was flushed from their lovemaking, her hair tossed around her face, her eyes shuttered and still sleepy. He felt his cock twitch with renewed interest, ready for another go. He wouldn't have believed himself capable of this kind of stamina if he wasn't experiencing it.

"You'll tempt me to get in trouble more often," he joked in response, crossing the room and hitting a switch on the wall, bringing the swirling water of the Jacuzzi to life.

"Oh," she murmured, eyeing the water. "That's a great idea."

She started to scuttle off of the bed, and he stopped her. She looked at him curiously, and he walked to the bed, slipping both arms beneath her and hauling her up next to him, delighting in her gasp of surprise.

"Brett—what are you doing?"

"Hopefully sweeping you off your feet," he said, looking into her eyes and carefully maneuvering down the teak steps that led to the inset tub. It was huge, even though he mostly used it by himself. As he lowered her to one of the wide benches, she groaned in appreciation as the hot, churning water covered her.

Brett's jaw stiffened with repressed desire as he saw her skin take on a sexy sheen of perspiration from the heat as she relaxed back, tempting bits of her body showing through the bubbles. She knew, and smiled back up at him with equal desire.

"Come on down here. You're too far away."

He didn't waste any time doing exactly as she asked.

11

LAUREN STRETCHED OUT on the divan by the window, her skin still pink from the Jacuzzi, feeling high on life. The massage, the sex, the aspirin, and the hot soak left her feeling more relaxed and happy than she'd been in a long time. Just twelve hours before her life had been a nightmare, but now she was floating on cloud nine.

Brett arrived through the door with breakfast, a tray filled with goodies and a steaming pot of coffee. As he set the tray down and took the seat opposite hers, she accepted the coffee he handed her.

"This is beautiful, but isn't it late? Don't you have to be down on the ranch?"

"Pete and I alternate Saturday and Sunday mornings. Today is my morning off."

She couldn't hold the weight of the cup, though her hand did throb less than it had the night before. During sex with Brett she hadn't felt any of it, she realized, smiling secretly to herself.

"What's that smile for?"

"Oh, I'm sorry. I know you were talking about the

ranch, but last night…this morning…" she drifted off and looked at him and he nodded.

"I know."

Grabbing a pastry, she broke the spell for a moment.

"Anyway, it's a new day. A fresh start. I want to help out even more, if I can."

"What do you mean?"

She looked out the window, suddenly finding it difficult to meet his gaze. They knew they were on the edge of something special, romantically speaking, but what was her place in his life otherwise? How did she fit in here?

"Well, after yesterday, I don't want to just keep mooching around here as your guest. I don't feel like your guest anymore," she equivocated, and chose her next words carefully. "I guess what I'm saying is that if I stay on the ranch, like you asked, I want to be part of it. I want to contribute. I don't just want to be your, um, you know, just the…I don't know if there's a word for it."

"Lover, girlfriend, best thing that ever happened to me. Take your pick," he offered, and her heart skipped a beat.

"Those are all nice options, but I'm not sure if that's how everyone else would see it."

"Why do you care? They'll know the truth about Marsha by now, and it will all settle down."

"Doesn't mean it will change how they look at

me, necessarily. I don't want to be a kept woman, Brett," she said, blushing slightly at the old-fashioned phrase, but that's what it amounted to. "I want to be part of your life, and that means being part of the ranch. And really learning about it, and you."

"Okay. What did you have in mind? What did you do before?"

"Well, I used to be an efficiency expert."

"What's that?"

"I consulted with companies, and looked at their management or production processes and tried to help them streamline to save money."

He frowned. "Sounds like a job that puts people out of work."

"Not always. Sometimes it actually added personnel. Many places try to cut corners by having their existing employees multitask, doing what isn't appropriate for them, and it causes a lot of problems that are expensive to fix later."

He acknowledged the point with a nod, silently waiting for her to continue.

"Anyway, I also did a lot of spatial reorganizing, helping people set up their business space or manage a home business, or just find a better flow in their lives."

He looked at her skeptically. "You think we need better…flow?"

She laughed. "It's not as New Age as it sounds. I actually have an engineering degree backing this up, thank you very much. Though the application to home organization was something I started myself. Wes hated it—he didn't want me doing anything that wasn't under his watch," she added, amazed at how simply and unemotionally she was able to share that.

Just saying it lifted a huge burden from her, as if those memories didn't weigh her down anymore. "I could help with things like that, you know. I've noticed some things that could be a bit more efficient," she offered carefully, not wanting to sound critical.

"I suppose we could work something out. I've been looking into an inventory problem," he said tentatively.

"Really? What kind of problem?"

He explained to her in short the trouble he'd been having.

"You think someone is ordering extra inventory, pocketing the extra cash they take to pay for them, and not ordering the materials?"

"That's what it looks like, but I don't have any evidence of who's doing it, since the orders were placed across the books, a little here, a little there. Some were even in my name, so whoever it is, they're falsifying the records, as well," he said.

She was pleased that he trusted her enough to confide in her, and didn't want to blow this connection between them.

"Who else has authority to make purchases?"

"Pete, Deke, Buck, Sherry. A few others have some minor authority for smaller stuff. I can't imagine any of them doing this. All of our purchases are pretty routine. These differences didn't even stand out for a while, because they looked normal, just a little bit over here and there, until I saw a pattern. I even wondered if it could be a computer glitch, if we were being hacked, which is why I brought in the forensic accountant."

"The guy from the other day."

"Yeah."

"Did he find anything?"

"Not so far. But I guess I have my suspicions."

"Can I ask who?"

He looked tense again, and she wished she could soothe away his worries.

"I'm keeping an eye on Deke. He did have a gambling problem years ago. He bought a new truck a while ago, seemed a little pricey for his income, but he said he got a good deal on a lease. I don't know…"

"It's hard when you have to suspect a friend." She didn't care much for Deke, but she knew he and Brett had a long history.

Brett nodded. "He was like an uncle when we were growing up. But he always had a kind of edgy side, especially when he was drinking."

"Will you bring charges when you find out who is responsible?"

Brett was pensive for a moment. "I don't know. I guess I'd have to discuss that with Pete. And I might be obliged to, legally speaking. I'd appreciate it if you'd keep this between us. No one else knows. I haven't even told Pete. I didn't want to get into it until I knew more."

"I won't say a word." Lauren was torn, thinking of her discussion with Pete, and he and Graciela's needing money to get her parents over the border. But did that necessarily mean they had been stealing from Brett? There was no way she could make an accusation like that without more proof.

"Thanks."

As they cleared off their breakfast, Lauren stood and stretched.

"You know, I don't know how much I could do, because I'm just a beginner myself, but maybe I could help out in the stables with the horses? I could help clean saddles, groom, work like that? I don't mind grunt work."

"Are you sure you wouldn't rather work in the house? Sherry could probably use some help, and you enjoyed working with Davie the other night. I know he's going to need a hand over the next few days getting ready for our *Día de los Muertos* barbeque. Apart from Christmas and Fourth of July, it's our biggest holiday event. There's a lot of decorating—Sherry gets guests involved with that—they should be starting today."

"I'd be happy to pitch in and help, but I'd like to do something on a daily, regular basis, too. I love working with the horses, and I could do the basics until I learn more. Maybe I could teach people to ride someday, or learn to train the horses myself."

Brett grinned. "You're really into it. A convert from Connecticut. Who would have thought?"

"I love it here. I really do. And I don't want to impose, but if I'm going to stay on the ranch, it has to be legitimately, earning my keep. It's the only way I can feel right about it. I want to be part of your life."

His expression warmed and he gathered her in his arms. "I want that, too. So horses it is, though we all pitch in for the barbeque, so we can ask Davie today what he needs done. I'll set you up with Deke for the stables."

"Thanks."

He kissed her forehead. "I guess it's time to shower and get to work then, both of us."

LAUREN'S BACK WAS ACHING, but it was a good ache. She stood and set down the saddle soap in her hand, propping her hands on a post and stretching her sore muscles. She loved this work, the manipulation of the soapy wax into the leather, the fragrant muskiness of it. She worked the saddles to a perfect shine, making sure no area was left untouched. It was a soothing task that Brett's wrangler had assigned her, and she didn't mind one bit.

As Brett promised, they'd all been busy for the last two days making paper flowers, sugar skulls and what seemed like an endless supply of decorations that were at once morbid and pretty, as well as food for an army, for the *Día de los Muertos* party. The ranch hands were stringing lights everywhere, and a small band of Mexican guitarists, friends of Davie's, were rehearsing in the main room. She could just faintly pick up the strains of the music from where she was in the stable.

It had been fun getting ready for the festivities and learning about the new holiday, but she was glad to finally find some time to spend in the barn, the place she could relax best.

"You actually look like you're enjoying yourself." She turned to find Sherry poised at the door of the tack shed, wearing riding clothes. She'd never seen Sherry down by the barns.

"I am. I like physical work. All that college for nothing," she joked, and Sherry laughed.

"You're fitting right in here."

"You sound surprised."

Sherry shook her head. "Nope, not really. Just glad you decided to give it another shot. I guess Brett must have been pretty convincing."

Lauren smiled. "Yeah. He can be that."

"I'm sneaking out for a break from the party planning and going for a ride. It's a beautiful day."

Lauren took in the leather boots Sherry wore.

Having bought her own, she recognized them, and realized they cost a pretty penny.

"Those are almost too attractive to wear riding."

Sherry grinned. "Aren't they though? I need to break them in. They cost a fortune, but Paul, my husband, told me to buy something I really wanted for my birthday, so I took him up on it. They are like sex for the feet, they feel so good on. Worth every cent."

"When was your birthday?"

"Last week."

"Oh. They didn't do anything here? Happy Birthday, belated."

"Davie wanted to make a cake, and I told him no. The last thing I need is more cake." She patted her stomach, but Lauren knew there wasn't an ounce of fat on her. She hoped she would be in as good shape when she was fifty.

"I suppose I should get some more riding clothes since I'll be around here for a while." *Or longer*, she thought happily. Hopefully.

"We'll go shopping. I know where you can get some deals."

"Great. Thanks," Lauren was happy to finally be treated with friendliness. Getting out and shopping sounded like fun.

"It's a date then. I'm glad we could be friends— I am sorry about the thing with Marsha. I thought I knew her, but then again, it seems I was wrong about most things."

"Believe me, you're not alone. Sometimes you just think you know someone, and then they turn on you. Can't blame yourself for being duped by people who pretend to be something they're not."

"I guess. Sounds like you know a little bit about it."

"Yeah. At least yours was a friend. I actually got married to someone like that."

Sherry moved away from the door, coming to sit on a bench beside where Lauren was working.

"Married! You were married? Does Brett know?" Sherry quickly slapped a hand over her mouth. "I'm sorry. None of my business."

Lauren laughed. "No, it's okay. Water under the bridge, mostly," she said with a sigh, realizing she hadn't heard back from Becky about whether the sale of the house had gone through. "I'm divorced, and yes, Brett knows. Believe me, we've decided on a *total* honesty policy from here on in."

Sherry put her head back and laughed, and Lauren looked at her curiously. "What?"

"Oh, honey, let me tell you what I tell my own daughters. Honesty is a part of any good relationship, but not total honesty. Couples don't need to know every little thing about each other. Sometimes the best thing for a relationship is a tightly kept secret."

"Well, maybe. I guess it depends on the secret."

"That's true." Sherry looked more serious, changing subjects again. "I've been worried about Brett lately. It seems like he has something on his mind, something other than you and him, or Marsha. I asked him, but he said everything was fine. I wondered if it had to do with that guy who came to meet him the other day, the suit. Brett's been pretty close-mouthed about who that was."

"I'm sure it was just some ranch business," Lauren hedged.

"I suppose, but normally Brett isn't so cagey about those things. Especially with me. I'm worried it could be a serious problem," Sherry said.

Lauren didn't say anything, focusing on switching the saddle she'd been working on with another one, trying to decide if Sherry was fishing. Was that what this wave of friendliness was about?

She tried to reason with herself. Lauren hated to be that cynical, but she really couldn't keep her suspicions at bay. Her gaze drifted down to Sherry's new boots. Certainly Brett paid his manager a good wage, but enough to afford that kind of designer luxury?

She tried to sound casual when she answered. If Sherry was the culprit, she wouldn't want to tip her off.

"I wouldn't be too concerned. If it were something serious, I'm sure he would tell you. Probably Davie too. I know he thinks the world of you both," she added for good measure, taking stock of Sherry's response with a slightly more critical eye.

"I suppose you're right." Sherry sighed. "I've been a little stressed out lately as well. I guess I'll head out on that ride. I'm going to go on over to the west ridge. I shouldn't be more than two hours. I've got water and my cell phone."

Lauren nodded, familiar with the protocol of sharing your route if you were going out riding alone.

"Have a good time."

For the rest of the day, she struggled with whether she should mention anything of it to Brett. She'd refrained from telling him about Pete and Graciela because after the moment had passed, nothing seemed to be happening, and she didn't want to make an enemy out of Pete. Pete should be the one to tell his brother what was happening, not her. She knew Brett planned to talk to him about Graciela, so hopefully they would straighten it out on their own.

On her way back to the house to clean up for dinner, she stopped by the guest quarters to drop off a hat that one of the vacationers had left in the barn. Ultimately, what did she have other than a few lame suspicions about Sherry or Graciela? Hardly enough to suggest to Brett that his manager or his staff could be ripping him off. Graciela didn't have access to the books, and somehow Lauren didn't see her as a clever computer hacker. Sherry had a good job with the ranch. Why would she risk it?

Amateur sleuthing was definitely not her forte.

For every person she suspected, she could just as easily talk herself out of it. Going to Brett would just cause undue tension unless she knew something for certain.

She turned the corner of the farthest corner of rooms, bumping into a cleaning cart left in the hall. Wasn't it a little late for housekeeping?

Moving around the edge of the cart, her belt snagged on a laundry bag knocking it to the floor. As she leaned to pick it up, she noticed something glittering among the towels that had spilled out. She picked up a woman's ring.

Lauren studied the ring; it had to be worth thousands of dollars. She looked at the laundry bag. Someone must have left it lying near their garbage and it had been picked up by mistake. Lauren put it in her pocket, knowing she had to give it to Brett so he could locate the owner immediately. If she'd lost a ring like that, she'd have a heart attack, even though it was probably insured.

Just as she was picking up the bag, someone came out of the room next to the cart, almost knocking her off her feet, but she caught herself in time.

"Graciela!"

Pete's girlfriend stared down at her in panic, and started talking so quickly in Spanish that Lauren had no idea what was going on, but the poor girl was obviously afraid she'd hurt her.

"No, no I'm fine. Promise. Isn't it late to be cleaning rooms?"

Graciela switched over to English. "I missed this one this morning, the Stephens, they sleep in late…so I come back to finish while they are at dinner," she explained. Lauren couldn't fault her for working hard.

"I'm sorry for messing up your cart. I came around the corner too fast and ran into it."

"You're fine?"

"I'm fine. Thanks, see you later."

The girl bid her a polite if cautious goodbye, and Lauren found the room she was looking for, returning the hat to its owner.

On her way back to the house, she fingered the ring in her pocket, musing. Graciela was mistaken—the Stephens, a couple visiting for their fortieth wedding anniversary, never slept in.

Every day they were the first ones up, raring to go, practically everyone commented on their energy and fun-loving spirits. In fact, Lauren had seen them that morning, heading over to a demonstration being given by a local Native American potter.

She took the ring from her pocket. Could Graciela have stolen the ring?

It was possible. And if Graciela was capable of that, could she be the one stealing money from the ranch as well? But how would she get access to the purchasing records?

And what if Lauren was wrong?

"Hey, what are you doing standing there in the dark?"

She whipped around to find Pete ambling up behind her, smiling. Suddenly it occurred to her what she had to do.

"Pete, hi. Listen, you got a minute? I need to talk to you. It's important."

"Sure. What's up?"

"C'mon over and let's sit down for a second," she said, walking to the front step.

Pete paused and then followed, looking guarded.

"Listen, Lauren, I know I said I would talk to Brett, but he has a lot on his mind right now, and we're handling things, Graciela and I, really. No need to pull him into it."

The discussion sparked Lauren's certainty that she was doing the right thing. Pete was obviously avoiding the issue, but he was also a grown man.

"Listen, Pete. There may be more going on than you think."

"What do you mean?"

"It's about Graciela. I bumped into her cleaning rooms about fifteen minutes ago—"

"At this time of day?"

"Right. That's what I thought. She said she'd missed the room early this morning because the Stephens slept in, but I know that's not true. And I found this in her cleaning cart."

Lauren opened her palm and showed Pete the ring, holding it up to the light. He whistled.

"I thought she might have picked it up accidentally while cleaning, but you know, I don't think it's likely any woman would leave this kind of expensive jewelry lying around."

Pete froze, and the silence between them thickened as he realized what she was saying.

"You think she stole it."

"What do you think? You told me she was sending money to get her parents brought here, but she's not, is she? She's stealing it. Did you know, Pete?"

Pete stood, his hands shoved in his pockets, and cursed. But what came out of his mouth was not what she expected. "Yes," he answered calmly. "I knew. I helped."

Lauren covered her mouth with her hands, shocked that what she'd suspected was true. "How could you do this to Brett?"

Pete's eyes widened. "He knows?"

"Of course he knows! He just doesn't know who, and would never suspect his own brother," she said accusingly.

"I know, I'm sorry. It's not like it's not my ranch, too, you know. Technically, half of all of this is mine," he said stubbornly, then seemed to wilt beneath her disbelieving stare.

"Then you should have asked for it outright, like

a man, not stolen it. You have to tell him. It's not right for him to live with suspecting everyone close to him. You will tell him," Lauren pressed.

"Now—I can't, not yet. These men, they're going to bring her parents over in two days—if she can get them the final payment. Give the ring to Brett, and I'll get her the money somehow. No more stealing, I promise. But she has to give them the money, Lauren. You don't understand. Once you are into these guys, you don't change your mind. They'll hurt her, or her parents, if we back out now."

Lauren didn't know what to do. What if Brett found out she knew, and hadn't told him? But what if she told him, and something went wrong, and people were hurt or died? Could she live with that?

"You've put me in a very bad spot, Pete. If Brett asks me, I'm not going to lie to him, but if you don't tell him, I will tell him myself. Tomorrow is the party, and if you don't come clean with him the very next day, I will. I promise you that."

His relief was clear in his expression, and he hugged her hard. "Thanks, Lauren. I promise I'll make this right, somehow. And when I do tell him, I'll keep you out of it. I don't want anything messing you two up. I know you're right for him, I just know it. Just like Graciela is right for me. It's why I had to risk everything to help her."

Lauren was uncomfortable with the easy rationalization on Pete's part, but then again, maybe he was right. She didn't feel right about her decision, but maybe it was the best she could do under the circumstances. She wished she'd never found the ring, never found out any of this. Was she making the right decision?

"Hey," Brett interrupted from the top of the porch. "What are you two doing out there? You're not making a play for my girl, are you, Pete?"

Brett stood there, looking at them, and Lauren felt so guilty. So much for total honesty. She didn't like this, not one bit. Pete said he would keep her out of it, but she planned to let Brett know her part in it, no matter what.

She would keep Pete's secret and after that she'd hope that Brett would understand. If not, then maybe they really weren't meant to be together. The idea made her heart sink.

"Nope, just having a little chat about the ranch. Leave any dinner for us?"

Pete ran up the steps, slapping his brother on the shoulder and going inside. Lauren hoped she could keep this secret for another two days, and forced a smile, meeting Brett by the door, the warm kiss he gave her wiping away most of her worry for the moment.

12

THE TRANSFORMATION of the ranch at sunset was beautiful on most days, but tonight, with the music from Spanish guitars, the starry desert sky and the twinkling lights strung everywhere, it was a magical place. Every visible space was decorated with bright paper flowers and colorful *ofrendas*, decorative tributes to the spirits being remembered. Two buffet tables were set up—one piled with barbequed meats coming straight off a smoking grill and side dishes, and another covered with desserts.

Lauren sat with her plate filled to the brim, a glass of wine at her side as she pondered how right it felt to celebrate the cycle of life and death in such a harsh yet stunning environment. She was learning from Brett what it mean to be a desert rancher, the hardy folks who took on the task, and how they succeeded through sheer will and discipline. But the same people knew how to celebrate and enjoy life, because they were completely in touch with how difficult it could be.

The festivities continued around them, dancing

everywhere, food everywhere, and a whoop went up from the crowd as a sassy young cowgirl snuck up behind a cowboy leaning on a post, talking with Brett. She daringly ripped the leather tag from the back of his jeans, running away playfully, waving the leather tag in the air.

"She ripped his jeans!" Lauren declared in surprise. Brett laughed as the ranch hand took off after the woman, who ran into the horse barn, checking with flirtatious looks to make sure he was following.

"It's just another way of picking someone up out here—especially if they rip it off with their teeth. She was actually being pretty polite considering," he explained.

"Back in Connecticut doing something like that wouldn't get you laid, but it might get you arrested," she joked, enjoying the hoot of laughter that went up from those who heard her. She'd never made an off-color joke in public before, and grinned at Brett, who grinned back.

Popping a bite of the spicy, sweet rib meat between her lips, she saw Brett take a few homemade tamales, some of which she'd even helped to make.

"This is so great—much better than a bowl full of Halloween treats and answering the door every five seconds."

"Have to agree with that," he said, attacking his tamale with relish.

"You did a great job. Davie and Sherry said you

worked your fingers to the bone—maybe I should make Lauren the party coordinator around here," Brett said cheerfully, a chorus of voices agreeing, and Lauren waved the playful suggestion away.

"I think I'll stick to working in the tack shed and stables for the moment, thanks. Though this was loads of fun," she responded. He lifted his glass, clinking it against hers, as others drifted off to dance and find more food.

"Speaking of horses, come here. There's something I need to talk to you about."

She set her plate down, too stuffed to eat any more anyway, and followed him down around the house to the old family barn where Brett and Pete kept their own horses.

"What's up?

"We'll just be a minute."

Shrugging, she walked alongside, leaving the din of the party behind them. Lauren stopped short at the door as he walked inside, spotting Macy in the stall closest to her.

"Why is she down here? Is she okay?" Lauren worried that maybe the horse was ill, and had to be taken out of the regular stables.

Brett took her by the hand, leading her down to where he'd moved Macy into the larger, more luxurious quarters beside Blaze.

"She's fine. Don't worry. Since you'll be staying here at the ranch, and if it's not too soon to say so,

I'm hoping you'll be part of the family someday." He swallowed, his voice catching slightly. "I thought you should have your horse down here, too."

It took her a moment to process, and he watched as realization and joy dawned on her face. He laughed when Macy nudged her shoulder, and Lauren squealed in delight, hugging the horse before she turned back to him.

"My horse? You're giving me Macy?"

"You love her, she loves you—it doesn't seem right to let anyone else ride her at this point. She's yours."

Lauren looked from him to the horse, covering her face with her hands as tears slipped down from her eyes, and he drew her up close to him.

"I want to give you everything, Lauren. I want to share everything with you. I don't want to scare you or make you feel pressured or—"

She lifted a hand to his lips. "Shh. None of that. This is perfect. I want to say it's too much, too soon, but there's no way I'm going to. I love her so much…"

Brett kissed her hair, pulling back to look down into her face, the question hanging in the air between them as she pushed up on tiptoe and kissed him gently.

"And you. It doesn't matter how much time we've been together. I know I love you, too."

Something inside of him clicked into place upon

hearing the words, and he wanted to throw his hat and yell it from the roof. Instead he kissed the life out of her, feeding the embers of passion between them until they were practically taking each other's clothes off in the barn, not that it mattered.

It was private. All he had to do was shut the door and they'd be perfectly free to experiment with those lead straps, like he'd been meaning to before. The idea of Lauren tied up and naked, vulnerable to every pleasure he could bring her, burnt a path through his bloodstream so hot he lost his breath. He framed her face with his hands and looked into her eyes, prepared to say the most important words he'd ever said in his life, and yet they were so easy, tripping from his lips as if it was the most natural thing in the world.

"I love you, too, Lauren. And that's the first time I've ever said that to any woman. I really believe you will be the last."

More happy tears trickled down her cheeks, and they ignored the snorting objections of the horses as Brett set about making the fantasy he'd been having reality.

"HEY, DID YOU HEAR anything else about your house?" Brett asked conversationally, but he studied her closely as they worked with the others cleaning up the food from the party before bed. The rest would be dealt with tomorrow.

She shook her head. "I'm figuring no news is good news, but if I don't hear from Becky in the next day or so, I suppose I'll have to call and see what's going on. If I have to go back, it won't be for long, though it won't be pleasant. I'd get to see my parents, which will be nice."

"Have you told them you're here?"

She nodded. "I called them a week or so ago, and reassured them I was still living. They seemed like they'd gotten over some of their miff about me taking off on my own. They're planning a trip, getting on with their lives. I think this has been good for them, too."

"I don't blame them for wanting to protect you, but I can see where too much protection isn't good for a child," he said.

"They loved me, and I was lucky for that, but I feel better knowing they can be with each other and not always have to be focusing on me, you know? I wondered how they would be together, as a couple, once I was gone."

"It's nice that you all worked it out."

"I'm glad, too," she agreed, her cheeks rosy from the wine, her eyes luminous.

He took a heavy stack of plates from her hands, and they went into the kitchen. "If you have to go back, would you like it if I went, too? I could meet them, maybe help out with things. With your house."

He was pretty transparent, and she smiled knowingly. "You mean you want to give my ex the evil eye? Feel free. And yes, if I have to go back, I would love you to come meet everyone, see where I grew up. I hope we can do that at some point. It's a wonderful place."

"Very different from here."

"Completely, but that's what makes both places so special."

"Well, even if you don't have to go back, why don't you invite your folks out here for a week? As family guests of course, not paying customers. I'd really like to get to know them—when you're ready for that," he added quickly.

She slid over and kissed his cheek. "I think that would be great, Brett. I want you to know my family, and I know they'll love you."

Speaking of family…she took a deep breath, looking around for Pete, but not seeing him anywhere. In fact, she hadn't really seen him or Graciela all evening. Were they off celebrating in private, or avoiding trouble?

"Did you and Pete talk today?"

She knew the answer already. Considering the weight of the conversation Pete was supposed to have with his brother, Lauren was pretty sure there would have been some aftershocks if Brett knew what was going on. Maybe Pete was waiting until after the festivities, but his absence was worrisome.

Brett shrugged. "I saw him earlier, but he seemed

preoccupied. We were all pretty busy, so no. He didn't talk about anything in particular, why?"

"I thought you two would talk about Graciela, you know, him dating her," she said, a sense of dread settling over her. She fumbled, almost dropping the glasses she carried.

"Hey, careful there. You all right?" Brett asked.

"I just realized we didn't see Pete all night. Did you? I'm a little concerned." she said, setting the glasses on the table.

"I'm sure he's fine—probably holed up with Graciela somewhere," Brett said casually.

She knew if he knew the entire story, he wouldn't be so nonchalant. She would have to tell him if Pete didn't. Thinking about that, she turned away. "I'll be right back, I'll go grab the rest of those trays on the last table."

He nodded, busy at the counter with Davie and Sherry and she slipped out. Once she was out the door, she ran quickly to the far building of staff quarters, finding Graciela's room.

The door was open, the place ransacked. Pete lay on the floor, unconscious and Lauren gasped, running to his prone form and finding a pulse, thank God.

"Pete?" She shook him gently, scanning over his body for injury but only finding a lump on the back of his head, "Pete, wake up!"

Patting her pocket, she realized she didn't have her cell phone with her at the party. It was in her room.

"I'll get help. I'll be right back."

She saw some people in the distance by one of the feed storage buildings. Squinting, she lifted her hand to her face. It looked like a fight. She bolted down the steps and across the dirt, hoping if it were just some partygoers getting randy they could stop their nonsense and help, but as she got closer, she saw two large men struggling with a woman who was fighting like a wildcat.

The men were trying to drag her into the side door of a large, black SUV, and there wasn't any time. She had to try to help the girl herself.

"Hey! You! Stop that. I've called the police, they're on their way. *Let her go*!" she yelled, hoping they believed her, and hoping someone heard her, though she was far away from the house. The two burly men turned away from the woman, and stared over at her.

"Graciela," she murmured, seeing Graciela break free and one of the men go after her.

The men must be the smugglers Pete was talking about. Her mind blank with fear, Lauren bolted in the opposite direction. Someone yanked her by the hair from behind and she cried out, falling backward.

As she hit the ground, her head cracked on something hard—the man's boot? Had he kicked her? Or was it a rock? Her vision blurred as he spoke to her in heavily accented English.

"Wrong place, wrong time, bitch." he said viciously, and did push her with his foot, on the hip where her almost-healed bruise protested. She bit her lip, not wanting to let him know he hurt her.

"I called the police…the ranch," she said through gritted teeth. "They know, help is coming…gave your license…"

He leaned down close. "Don't bullshit me. Our van doesn't have a plate on the back. Get up."

He hauled her up by the armpits; her knees buckled as he yanked her along. The pain cleared her mind and she shoved him and got away, screaming for help. If the thug thought he was taking her somewhere, he had another thing coming. She wasn't going to go easily.

It was the last thing she thought until a blinding pain shattered the night.

BRETT LEFT THE HOUSE, wondering where Lauren could have gone. He thought she might have gotten talking to someone, but the yard was empty, and the trays she'd said she was going to get were still on the table.

He heard truck tires ripping out away from the ranch, and saw taillights disappearing down the main road. He remembered Lauren's concern about Pete— had she gone to find him?

Brett checked his brother's room, and asked Davie and Sherry, but they hadn't seen him. Jogging down to the staff quarters, he saw Graciela's room open, and found Pete standing in the middle of the room, dazed. Something was very wrong.

He grabbed his brother by the shirt, hauling him in close, releasing his hold when he saw Pete's pale complexion and dilated pupils.

"What happened?"

"I was here…tried to talk Graciela out of going, but someone came in, hit me—hard." Pete groaned. "I don't feel too well," he said, his knees giving way, and Brett caught him before he hit the deck again and put him back down in the one chair left upright.

"What's going on, Pete? Where's Graciela? Where the hell is Lauren?" Brett asked in fear.

"What do you mean? I don't know—" the color faded from his brother's face.

"Just cut the shit, Pete. I know you're seeing this woman, so tell me now. *Now.* Who hit you? Did they take Graciela and Lauren?"

Brett loved his brother, but he was as close to losing it as he'd ever been. He'd go through whatever, or whoever, he had to, to get to her—including his little brother. Pete took a deep breath, meeting his brother's eyes and giving him the basic rundown.

"Yeah. I don't know how Lauren got involved, but she knew— I was out cold. Did she come down here?"

"That's my guess. I want to know what's going on—all of it. I'm calling the sheriff."

"No! Don't—not yet. That will make things worse. I've never been there, but I have some idea where they might be."

Brett hauled his little brother back up to his feet, dragging him along as they headed for the truck. "Tell me on the way."

"Okay, okay. But no cops. They'll send her back, Brett. We can handle this ourselves."

The anguish in Pete's voice might have touched him if he weren't scared to death about where Lauren was, and who had her, and why.

"What are you talking about?"

"Graciela. She's…not legal. She got involved with some smugglers, trying to get her parents over the border. She's been trying to get enough money to pay them, but she fell short, and she had to meet them tonight, but she didn't have the cash. I told her I'd get it for her, but we ran out of time. They came here. That's who took them."

Deep inside Brett was furious, but it all roiled beneath the deadly calm he had to maintain. He had to keep a cool head to help Lauren; that was all that mattered now.

"How the hell did an illegal alien end up working here?"

Pete had the grace to look ashamed as they climbed into the truck. "I met her before you hired her. I fell for her at first sight, and I wanted to help, to give her a job, to have her around."

Brett remembered, grimacing. "You processed her job application. But there really wasn't one, was there?"

"No. I faked it all. Lied. I'm sorry," he said weakly. "But I love her. I want to marry her. We have to find a way not to send her back."

"That's not my first concern right now, and it shouldn't be yours. She might not survive to tell about it."

"Oh God," Pete moaned.

Brett was even more concerned now that he knew what was happening. These two women were in real danger. He tried to keep from imagining the worst as he slammed the truck in gear and tore off down the road in the direction Pete instructed, to the meeting spot where he and Graciela were supposed to have gone earlier. Regardless of Pete's worries about his girlfriend being deported, Brett got on his cell phone, immediately calling the Border Patrol and informing them of the situation.

As he outlined what he knew to the agent on the phone, he sped down the road toward the shed trying to tamp down his worries. The agent warned him to stay put and they'd find the abandoned building where the smugglers were supposed to have been holed up.

"To hell with that," Brett muttered to himself as finished the call. He wasn't about to step aside, not when Lauren was at risk, not to mention everything else dear to him. What would happen to the ranch? What about Pete? Would he be put in jail for his role in this? What if the women were hurt, or killed?

No, he couldn't consider that.

"It's going to take the agents at least a half hour to get here, and we may not have that kind of time. It's up to us."

Brett hit the gas. "Why would they have taken Lauren?"

Pete looked out the window. "She was just in the wrong place at the wrong time, Brett. She knew something was going on because I told her. I made her keep it a secret though. Don't blame Lauren."

Brett shook his head, disbelieving. How could Lauren have kept something this important from him? Didn't any of them know what danger they had put their lives in?

"I'm sorry, Brett. This is all my fault. I should have come to you sooner. Lauren told me to. She said from the beginning that we should have come to you, and she tried to make me," he said.

Brett didn't know what to think.

"I don't know if I can live with myself if anything happens to either of them, Brett," Pete choked out.

Brett's hands tightened on the steering wheel. Now was not the time to be arguing with Pete, who was clearly suffering enough for his bad decisions. Hopefully Graciela and Lauren wouldn't suffer even worse, for all of their sakes.

"No one's going to hurt those girls, Pete. Though what happens to Graciela after the authorities show up, I can't promise."

Pete nodded miserably, and Brett sped up, hoping he could get there in time.

LAUREN SAT NEXT TO GRACIELA, glaring at the men across the room who were stuffing their faces with takeout hamburgers that they'd picked up in town. They didn't even offer the women a sip of water.

She and Graciela were both tied tightly to wooden chairs. Her head was throbbing, and she was fairly sure she had a concussion. She searched her memory, trying to remember how to tell, but the pain and her blurred vision were likely symptoms. Weak with fear and pain, she struggled to stay awake.

She glanced over at Graciela who remained unconscious. Her beautiful face was streaked with tears. She'd been unable to stop crying, and finally one of the men had gotten fed up and struck her so hard she'd passed out and hadn't woken up yet.

Grunting, Lauren shuffled in her chair, trying to get their attention. If she could ask to use the bathroom, maybe she could find a window or something. It was better than sitting here waiting for the inevitable.

She didn't know what the inevitable was. The men had made several phone calls and spoke in Spanish.

"What's your problem?" the one man growled, his gaze cold.

She mumbled against her gag, trying to tell him with her expression and tones that she needed to get up, and finally he pushed his chair back and approached, ripping the cloth out of her mouth. She sucked in air through dry lips, her mouth feeling like cotton, but it was good to breathe easily.

"I need to use the bathroom," she croaked, hoping he bought it.

Instead, he barked out a laugh. "You think I'm stupid? You stay put. You don't move, or you'll be like your friend," he promised softly, dragging a finger down the curve of her jaw, making her shudder.

"I don't feel well...I really need to go," she insisted, sucking in a breath when he grabbed a handful of hair and yanked her head back sharply.

"Too bad," he said, then he smiled, and it chilled her straight through. "The bathroom is upstairs, *chica*. If I take you up there, you might not come down for a while. You're very pretty," he said salaciously. She froze, understanding his intentions all too clearly. Suddenly, her plan to insist on using the bathroom seemed like a very bad idea.

"Hey! Hands off the merchandise," his friend warned. "Her old man won't pay for her if she's damaged, and neither will anyone else."

"I can make it not show," the man said leering at her.

"You lay a hand on me and you'll be sorry," she threatened, knowing her father was probably pulling out all of the stops to find her, even if Brett hadn't realized what was happening yet. When these jerks had demanded she give them her family's information, she'd been more than happy to share, leading them along. They had no idea of the connections her father had, or that he'd never let them take her anywhere. In the meantume, she just had to keep herself alive.

"Your father pays us for you, it makes everything easier. Otherwise we have to get you both back over the border and sell you there. He pays us, we leave you here, someone finds you sooner…or later." He grinned. "We make sure we have our money and leave the country before we tell them where you are. Otherwise, you come with us, and we get our money one way or the other."

"You're risking a lot kidnapping an American citizen, you know."

"No one will care who you are south of the border, *chica*. White women, especially nice white women like you, can fetch much more than someone like her." He nodded dismissively at Graciela. "We won't bother bringing her along, if it comes down to it. Makes things more complicated."

"You'd kill her?" Lauren asked, horrified.

"She didn't pay us, so she deserves what she gets. If your father pays, you both may live. It's quicker, easier," he explained, as if she were supposed to admire how clever his plan was.

"It'll never work. My father will contact the FBI. He won't give into this," she promised, wishing she could spit in his face, but her mouth was like sandpaper.

"That will be very unfortunate for you, and for her."

Lauren bit her lip almost drawing blood. How the hell would she get out of this? She hoped she wasn't counting too heavily on her father to bail her out, but she couldn't think of any other way to survive this. As stupid as it was, she felt her eyes burn with tears as she realized what else this would prove to her parents: that the first time she'd gone out on her own, really on her own, she ended up living with a guy she picked up on the side of the highway, and then she got kidnapped by smugglers. If she lived through this, she was going to have a hard time convincing her parents how competent and independent she was.

The smuggler left her in peace and didn't replace the gag, thank God. What a mess she'd gotten herself into.

Her eye caught a movement outside the dirty window, or so she thought. It was probably just a reflection of light from the highway nearby. She slid her gaze to her captors, who had returned their attention to their food and conversation, and she looked back as if she were watching the television in the corner. Yes! Saw it again…her vision was still not completely clear, but there was definitely something, or someone, out there.

Then she saw him—Brett—his face just outside the window by the door as he made his way along the side of the house. How had he found her? It seemed like a miracle. It didn't matter. He was here; there was hope.

He made some kind of motion to her in the window and she tried to figure out what he was telling her. Why didn't he just call the police, get help? He shouldn't take these guys on. They had guns. She tried to shake her head no, to warn him, but she didn't want to draw attention to him, either.

It was too late. He was moving toward the door, and she reacted, going on instinct, lurching herself to the side and tipping the chair off balance. She braced herself for the crash of the impact. This was going to hurt.

It did.

It also drew the attention of the men to her as they cursed loudly in Spanish and stood from the table, crossing the room menacingly, leaving their weapons about ten feet away. At the same time, Brett crashed through the front door, rifle in hand. He aimed it at the two men who lunged for their own weapons, but one shot from Brett to the floor in front of the first guy's foot froze them in place.

Lauren groaned, her new position sideways on the floor a painful one. She might have broken her arm.

"You—untie them *now*," Brett ordered, training the rifle at them, his hold steady.

The men stood there belligerently, staring Brett down. "Forget it, honcho. No way you can take us both, and even if you do get these girls out the door, then it will just be us and you."

The sound of tires scratching the dirt road filled the room as flashing lights filled the room, and Brett smiled.

"Wrong again, amigo."

As agents swarmed the room, Brett put his hands up, and identified himself as they took his gun. Lauren yelled to them, telling them it was the other men, who were already on the floor, being cuffed, glaring and cursing. After a brief discussion with the agent who had grabbed Brett's gun, they allowed him to come over to her. She didn't bother to choke back her tears of pain and relief as he removed her bindings ever so gently then drew her up against him.

"I'd say this is taking your life of adventure a little too far, darlin'," he said, hugging her lightly, releasing her when she winced, and then EMTs entered the room.

Lauren was glad to see they were attending to Graciela first, who had just regained some consciousness. She wasn't dead, thank goodness. Everything was going to be all right.

"Brett, I'm so sorry, so much…"

"Shh. We have time for that later. Right now these good people are going to get you to the hospital in Tucson, all right? I won't be far behind."

She nodded, tears coming far too easily. All of this was her fault, and Brett had to know that, too. Now that she was free, she glanced around the room and saw Pete break through the doorway, rushing over to Graciela and hugging her tightly. The EMTs asked him to back away, and his face was so haggard, so pained, he looked several years older.

Two strapping young EMTs helped her on to the gurney. She saw the relief, pain and betrayal that played in Brett's eyes as he regarded Pete. She wondered how he would ever be able to forgive her.

13

"ARE YOU SURE YOU DON'T want me to come out there? You sound like you need me," Becky said, concern evident in her voice.

"No, I'm fine. You have too much going on to come out and babysit me," Lauren said wearily, exhausted from the two-hour conversation it took to convince her parents not to fly out immediately either.

She caught her image in the mirror. Not pretty. She was pale still, banged up and bruised, with six stitches over her left temple. They'd had to shave a little of her hair out of the way there, which was just stupid looking. Barbie Frankenstein.

She'd been back at the ranch for two days—three days after the kidnapping. As it turned out, her father hadn't even gotten the ransom demand until after it was all over. He'd been out of town and hadn't been checking his messages. He was frantic of course, when he did get the calls. He'd called in every favor that he could to get the FBI to prioritize the case, only to find out that everything was already over with and Lauren was safe and sound.

Not that that saved her from a very long lecture on all the reasons she should come back home.

As she looked out the window of her room—the one she'd stayed in before she'd started spending nights with Brett—she couldn't think of a reason to go home. She also couldn't think of a reason she should stay.

Brett had gone to Tucson with the business of getting Pete's ass out of the legal jam he'd gotten into with Graciela, and though he'd been to the hospital with her and left a few clipped messages on her cell, she couldn't imagine that there was much left to say between them.

His life had been turned upside down, and she had been part of it. After promising him truth, she'd lied. She couldn't imagine how they'd get past that, considering his recent past, and she couldn't blame him.

He was supposed to be home in a few hours, and she figured she'd be gone by then.

"So what are you going to do?" Becky brought her back to the moment.

"I don't know. Stick to the original plan, just a few weeks off course. Head west, find a place to live, a job."

"You should try talking it out. Sounds like you two had a good thing going."

"He's been through enough. I mean, think about it. The woman he was going to marry, his brother, one of his employees and now me, have all lied to him within a few weeks' time, all with horrible consequences. He's been cheated on, stolen from and almost shot himself taking on those smugglers. Which never would have happened if I'd told him sooner. Do you think that's going to leave him open to discussion?"

"I guess I see your point, though you had solid reasons for doing what you did. There was no way you could know it would turn out like this."

"Maybe so, but that's kind of beside the point. I'm going to take off in a little bit. I'll let you know where I end up."

"Okay. Be safe."

"Thanks." Lauren cut off the call, pressing her hand where the tight ache in her throat had been bothering her for days, especially every time she thought about leaving. She didn't know if it was the right thing, but it seemed to be the best way to save everyone the most pain and drama. Brett had been through enough, and she'd save him telling her to go.

Hauling her bag up over her shoulder, she took one last look at the room and walked down, grateful that only Davie was in the kitchen, getting ready for dinner. He glanced up, his brow furrowing.

"You going somewhere?"

"I—I think it's time for me to leave," she said softly. The knowing look Davie sent her way, full of concern and sympathy she didn't deserve, threatened to let loose the dam.

"Brett won't be happy." Davie frowned. "You only have another hour or so of daylight. Why leave now? Wait until morning."

"I think it's better if I just go. I'll be fine. I don't want to cause him any more trouble than he has already right now. You know, sometimes things just don't work out," she said, her voice trembling as he nodded quietly, his dark eyes troubled as she rushed from the room.

It would have been easier just to go to her car and leave, but there was something important she had to do first. Forcing pleasant hellos to some of the guests she knew, she responded briefly to their concerned inquiries as she walked down through the riding stable, letting Deke know she wouldn't be available for work from now on, and headed over to the private stables.

The horses stomped around a little in reaction to her, and she saw that Brett's horse Blaze had his head leaned over where Macy was nuzzling him. Her eyes teared up.

"You two make a great couple," she said with a laugh petting Macy's nose and hugging her neck.

Macy neighed softly in response, as if asking her what was wrong.

"You're such a sensitive girl. I hate to leave you, but I know Brett loves you, too, everyone does, and

you'll be fine. I'll miss you horribly, though," she
whispered, petting the soft, bristly coat of the gentle
horse one final time. She left the barn and made her
way down to the lower outbuildings where her car
hadn't been started for weeks.

When she settled into the driver's seat, it felt familiar and she sat there for a moment, reassessing
her life. She'd had a minor detour was all—gained
some experience, some wisdom, and now she'd be
on her way. Determined not to cry again, she turned
the ignition, holding her breath, but her car purred
to life as reliably as it always did. A message from
fate, maybe, that this was the right decision.

"Well, here we go," she said aloud, ignoring the
sights around her, not even thinking about the steep
canyons that lay ahead as she drove down the dusty
road leading from the ranch.

As she turned up the curving highway that Brett
had driven down that first day, her thoughts were fo-
cused on the road. She had her life in front of her,
stretching out the same way, an open highway.

However, when she thought about what came next,
she couldn't picture anything other than Brett. Their
last time making love in the barn came back to her,
how daring and amazing it had been, and how uninhibited she'd learned to be. How he'd told her he loved
her.

Lauren buzzed around a corner, seeing nothing
but sky and the other side of the canyon, and she

realized she was about halfway up already, navigating the curves like a pro.

Slowing down, she was stunned by the fact that she wasn't afraid. She wasn't going too slow or inching around every steep part of the road like a mouse. She was simply and confidently driving.

Moving forward.

She and Brett had had a good thing—for about three weeks. She'd walked away from a seven-year marriage with less pain than she felt walking away from Brett. She'd certainly never felt the emotions and the attachment to Wes that she'd developed for Brett in this short time, but she knew that was okay.

Brett, the ranch, her life there—it was freedom. Not only had he shown her what real love was, he'd helped her realize her own potential. All of the jittery fears and reservations she'd had through her life melted away. After all, she could have stayed back and not helped when she saw the men taking Graciela, but who knew if they ever would have found Graciela in time?

Instead, she'd charged in, and while that might have been stupid, she hadn't been afraid. At least, not at first. And she'd even accepted the pain of crashing to the hard floor to distract the kidnappers from Brett—helping him save them. Working together, a team.

She'd learned to stand up for herself, to ride a

horse and to drive these damned roads. She wasn't afraid of any of it anymore.

So why was so she afraid of facing Brett? Of his possible rejection? Of fighting for what they had together?

Easy answer: she wasn't afraid. Not one little bit.

A lightbulb went off in her head, and everything became clear. She was running away, and it was time to stop. Of all the risks she'd taken, she was going to take one more and fight for what they had. No more running away. Just like Brett had said: running away from your problems was never the right choice.

Finding a small patch of dirt on the side of the road, she spun the car decisively around, heading back down the mountain. Her heart fluttered with excitement, the tightness in her throat vanished.

With any luck, she'd be back before he was, and they'd have a good, honest talk about what happened. She'd had her reasons for keeping Pete's confidence, though if she could do it differently now, she would. The main thing was that she and Brett had made a promise to each other—they'd said they loved each other—and she wasn't going to let that go so easily.

As she turned one very sharp corner, the Toyota Corolla started to cough. She pushed the gas, but nothing happened as the car glided slowly to a stop, resting next to a tall canyon wall.

"Incredible," she said, raising a hand to her forehead as she peeked out from between her fingers at the needle pointing directly to E.

She was out of gas.

BRETT WAS SO TIRED he couldn't focus. All he wanted to see at the moment was Lauren. In very short order, that's exactly what he'd be doing.

When he'd seen her tied to that chair, the blood gushing down her face and the guns sitting on the table, he'd lost years off his life. All that mattered was saving her, although she'd probably saved him as well, creating a distraction when he'd broken through the door.

When he'd gone to the hospital, he'd found out pretty quickly—and much to his aggravation—that nonrelatives didn't have much access to patients outside of visiting hours. Finding the time to see Lauren had been a challenge, considering how much straightening out there was to do with the police, and the Border Patrol, regarding Pete and Graciela. Finally he'd found a good lawyer to handle their case. It had all sucked up two days like nothing. And all he wanted, all that time, was to get back to his girl.

He drove back to the ranch using the eastern access roads, a quicker if steeper approach. He was probably driving just a little recklessly, the lights of his home in the distance, and Lauren. They had a lot to talk about, but right now he just needed to see her and hold her.

Minutes later, he drove up front. Pete would be home tomorrow—with Graciela, who was his wife now. He and Brett and their lawyer had arranged for a quick but legal marriage, so she couldn't be deported. How to get her family here was another question altogether. There was some other red tape to sort through, some fees and fines, but it would more or less work out. Brett would help, but at the moment he had to get his own life in order.

Busting in the front door he saw Sherry and Davie's eyes widen in surprise. "Hi. I know, I'm sorry. I'll catch you both up later. Where's Lauren?"

Davie and Sherry shared an apprehensive look.

"What's wrong? Did the hospital call? Did something happen? Why didn't anyone call me?" he demanded.

His mind zoomed immediately to the worst and Sherry put her hands up in a gesture he hoped was reassurance as she came over to him.

"No, no. She's fine. Nothing's wrong. She's just not here."

"Where is she?"

Sherry took a deep breath, looking very pained and cast a glance at Davie who took a step forward.

"She left a little over an hour ago. She looked very sad. I think she feels responsible, and thought she should go. She seemed to feel things were over with you, and she was trying to make it easier."

"She didn't see you, or hear from you, and I think

she might have taken that as a message," Sherry added.

Brett ran a hand over his face.

"Jesus. I left some messages telling her to stay put and I'd be back soon."

Sherry's eyebrows raised. "Well, yes, that must have been very reassuring," she said with subtle sarcasm.

"Sherry, there's been so much going on, I could barely keep track. I had the authorities to deal with, and a marriage to arrange—"

"What?"

"Pete and Graciela. We managed to keep Pete from being arrested, though that's not quite over yet. I'm lucky I made it back today, but I…" He sighed, deflated. "I thought she'd wait."

Sherry looked at him with a sparkle in her eye. "Well, she couldn't have gotten very far. You know she hates those winding roads."

"Good call. I'm gone. Don't wait up."

Sherry and Davie yelled good luck, but he barely heard them as he raced back to the truck. He'd catch her, and they'd have that talk, and he'd bring her back. Simple as that.

The sun had set and the roads were dark, and while he and Sherry had joked about Lauren driving so slow she'd be no trouble to catch, he was worried. These roads were difficult for people unfamiliar with them, especially at night. With her fear of heights, if Lauren had been upset or rushing, they could be deadly. Serious concern lodged in his chest until he saw a car parked on the other side of the road—Lauren's Corolla.

She popped out of the car, spotting him, and he pulled up alongside, massively relieved.

"Break down?" he asked, his heart thundering but he kept his tone casual.

She paused for a moment, looking down at the dirt, then back at him again. She nodded, playing along, stuffing her hands in her pockets, shrugging. He smiled. She had her hat on.

"Ran out of gas."

"From what I heard, you're going in the wrong direction," he observed. "Weren't you heading out?"

"I changed my mind. Realized running away wasn't the way to go when there's something worth fighting for back home."

Home. Her use of the word seemed so right. It really had felt like home again with her there. They were both crazy to be parked on the road as it grew dark, but things needed to be said, now. He slid out of the truck, gathering her into his arms.

"Why'd you leave in the first place?"

"I didn't think you'd want me there. None of this with the kidnapping would have happened if I'd told you what I'd learned about Pete earlier," she confessed miserably. "I just couldn't believe you'd want me to stay. How could you?"

He drew back, looking at her with astonishment. "How could I not? Lauren, I told you I loved you. And I do. I don't take things like that lightly."

"Me, either, but…I've just been so wrong."

"I'll admit I wished you'd told me, but Pete said that he asked you to keep the secret, and that you were afraid, as he was, that lives might be at stake. No one knew it would be yours. The thought of losing you…." He couldn't quite finish, and instead hugged her tightly to him, reassuring himself that she really was there.

"I'm so sorry, Brett. I just…I don't know. But when I was driving up the roads, and I realized I wasn't afraid anymore, I knew why. It's because of you, and because I love you, and that was worth coming back and fighting for."

He kissed her hair. "You won't have to fight terribly hard. I'm just so glad I found you."

"When I didn't hear from you, and you sounded so clipped in your messages, I guess I didn't trust what was between us yet. I do now."

"I'm sorry. I was going crazy to get back to you, but the government hauled Pete in, and Graciela. There were legal issues that had to be handled right then, and we managed to sneak in a quick wedding so they couldn't deport her—"

"Pete and Graciela got married?"

Brett smiled, pushing her hair back and wincing as he noted the stitches at her temple.

"Yesterday. There are still some problems that will have to be ironed out, but the worst is over."

"I'm sorry I wasn't there for you when you got back. I should have trusted us more."

"Well." He smiled, looking back at where her car was parked. "I'm glad you decided to turn around. I'm so crazy about you I can't think straight. No matter what's going on around us, no matter where we are, all I really need to have is you."

"I feel the same way," she murmured, looking into his eyes.

His lips were warm on hers as they sank into a kiss sealing the promises between them, and as a car whisked by they broke apart.

"Guess we'd better get back home," he said huskily, the idea of home, for good this time, hitting him square in the heart.

"What about my car?"

"We'll come back, get it tomorrow. Right now, I want you with me by my side. Permanently."

"I like that plan." She grinned, linking her fingers with his as they went over to the truck. "I'm lucky you decided to stop and pick me up."

He laughed, leaning in to kiss her as she climbed inside.

"I guess that goes for both of us."

* * * * *

Welcome to cowboy country...

Turn the page for a sneak preview of
TEXAS BABY
by
Kathleen O'Brien.
An exciting new title from Harlequin
Superromance for everyone
who loves stories about the West.

Harlequin Superromance—
where life and love weave together in emotional
and unforgettable ways.

CHAPTER ONE

CHASE TRANSFERRED his gaze to the road and identified a foreign spot on the horizon. A car. Almost half a mile away, where the straight, tree-lined drive met the public road. He could tell it was coming too fast, but judging the speed of a vehicle moving straight toward you was tricky.

It wasn't until it was about two hundred yards away that he realized the driver must be drunk…or crazy. Or both.

The guy was going maybe sixty. On a private drive, out here in ranch country, where kids or horses or tractors or stupid chickens might come darting out any minute, that was criminal. Chase straightened from his comfortable slouch and waved his hands.

"Slow down, you fool," he called out. He took the porch steps quickly and began walking fast down the driveway.

The car veered oddly, from one lane to another, then up onto the slight rise of the thick green spring grass. It just barely missed the fence.

"Slow down, damn it!"

He couldn't see the driver, and he didn't recognize this automobile. It was small and old, and couldn't have cost much even when it was new. It was probably white, but now it needed either a wash or a new paint job or both.

"Damn it, what's wrong with you?"

At the last minute, he had to jump away, because the idiot behind the wheel clearly wasn't going to turn to avoid a collision. He couldn't believe it. The car kept coming, finally slowing a little, but it was too late.

Still going about thirty miles an hour, it slammed into the large, white-brick pillar that marked the front boundaries of the house. The pillar wasn't going to give an inch, so the car had to. The front end folded up like a paper fan.

It seemed to take forever for the car to settle, as if the trauma happened in slow motion, reverberating from the front to the back of the car in ripples of destruction. The front windshield suddenly seemed to ice over with lethal bits of glassy frost. Then the side windows exploded.

The front driver's door wrenched open, as if the car wanted to expel its contents. Metal buckled hideously. Small pieces, like hubcaps and mirrors, skipped and ricocheted insanely across the oyster-shell driveway.

Finally, everything was still. Into the silence, a plume of steam shot up like a geyser, smelling of rust and heat. Its snakelike hiss almost smothered the low, agonized moan of the driver.

Chase's anger had disappeared. He didn't feel anything but a dull sense of disbelief. Things like this didn't happen in real life. Not in his life. Maybe the sun had actually put him to sleep....

But he was already kneeling beside the car. The driver was a woman. The frosty glass-ice of the windshield was dotted with small flecks of blood. She must have hit it with her head, because just below her hairline a red liquid was seeping out. He touched it. He tried to wipe it away before it reached her eyebrow, though, of course, that made no sense at all. Her eyes were shut.

Was she conscious? Did he dare move her? Her dress was covered in glass, and the metal of the car was sticking out lethally in all the wrong places.

Then he remembered, with an intense relief, that every good medical man in the county was here, just behind the house, drinking his champagne. He found his phone and paged Trent.

The woman moaned again.

Alive, then. Thank God for that.

He saw Trent coming toward him, starting out at a lope, but quickly switching to a full run.

"Get Dr. Marchant," Chase called. "Don't bother with 911."

Trent didn't take long to assess the situation. A fraction of a second, and he began pulling out his cell phone and running toward the house.

The yelling seemed to have roused the woman. She opened her eyes. They were blue and clouded with pain and confusion.

"Chase," she said.

His breath stalled. His head pulled back. "What?"

Her only answer was another moan, and he wondered if he had imagined the word. He reached around her and put his arm behind her shoulders. She was tiny. Probably petite by nature, but surely way too thin. He could feel her shoulder blades pushing against her skin, as fragile as the wishbone in a turkey.

She seemed to have passed out, so he put his other arm under her knees and lifted her out. He tried to avoid the jagged metal, but her skirt caught on a piece and the tearing sound seemed to wake her again.

"No," she said. "Please."

"I'm just trying to help," he said. "It's going to be all right."

She seemed profoundly distressed. She wriggled in his arms, and she was so weak, like a broken bird. It made him feel too big and brutish. And intrusive. As if touching her this way, his bare hands against the warm skin behind her knees, were somehow a transgression.

He wished he could be more delicate. But he smelled gasoline, and he knew it wasn't safe to leave her here.

Finally he heard the sound of voices, as guests began to run around the side of the house, alerted by Trent. Dr. Marchant was at the front, racing toward them as if he were forty instead of seventy. Susannah was right behind him, her green dress floating around her trim legs.

"Please," the woman in his arms murmured again. She looked at him, the expression in her blue eyes lost and bewildered. He wondered if she might be on drugs. Hitting her head on the windshield might account for this unfocused, glazed look, but it couldn't explain the crazy driving.

"Please, put me down. Susannah... The wedding..."

Chase's arms tightened instinctively, and he froze

in his tracks. She whimpered, and he realized he might be hurting her. "Say that again?"

"The wedding. I have to stop it."

* * * * *

Be sure to look for TEXAS BABY,
available September 11, 2007,
as well as other fantastic Superromance titles
available in September.

HARLEQUIN *Super Romance*®

Welcome to Cowboy Country...

TEXAS BABY

by *Kathleen O'Brien*

#1441

Chase Clayton doesn't know what to think.
A beautiful stranger has just crashed his
engagement party, demanding that he not
marry because she's pregnant with his baby.
But the kicker is—he's never seen her before.

Look for TEXAS BABY and other fantastic
Superromance titles on sale September 2007.

Available wherever books are sold.

HARLEQUIN® *Super Romance*®

**Where life and love weave together
in emotional and unforgettable ways.**

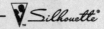

REQUEST YOUR FREE BOOKS!

2 FREE NOVELS PLUS 2 FREE GIFTS!

HARLEQUIN®

Blaze®

Red-hot reads!

Silhouette® Desire

Don't miss the first book in the
BILLIONAIRE HEIRS trilogy

THE KYRIAKOS VIRGIN BRIDE
#1822

BY TESSA RADLEY

Zac Kyriakos was in search of a woman pure both
in body and heart to marry, and he believed that Pandora
Armstrong was the answer to his prayers. When Pandora
discovered that Zac's true reason for marrying her was
because she was a virgin, she wanted an annulment. Little
did she know that Zac was beginning to fall in love with
her and would do anything not to let her go....

On sale September 2007 from Silhouette Desire.

BILLIONAIRE HEIRS:
They are worth a fortune...but can they be tamed?

Also look for
THE APOLLONIDES MISTRESS SCANDAL
on sale October 2007
THE DESERT BRIDE OF AL SAYED
on sale November 2007

Available wherever books are sold.

ATHENA FORCE

Heart-pounding romance and thrilling adventure.

Professional negotiator Lindsey Novak is faced with her biggest challenge—to buy back Teal Arnett, a young woman with unique powers. In the process Lindsey uncovers a devastating plot that involves scientists from around the globe, and all of them lead to one woman who is bent on destroying Athena Academy...at any cost.

LOOK FOR

THE GOOD THIEF

by Judith Leon

Available September wherever you buy books.

HARLEQUIN®

COMING NEXT MONTH

#345 KIDNAPPED! Jo Leigh
Forbidden Fantasies

She had a secret desire to be kidnapped and held against her will.... But when heiress Tate Baxter's fantasy game turns out to be all too real, can sexy bodyguard Michael Caulfield put aside his feelings and rescue her in time?

#346 MY SECRET LIFE Lori Wilde
The Martini Dares, Bk. 1

Kate Winfield's secrets were safe until hottie Liam James came along. Now the sexy bachelor with the broad chest and winning smile is insisting he wants to uncover the delectable Katie—from head to toe.

#347 OVEREXPOSED Leslie Kelly
The Bad Girls Club, Bk. 3

Isabella Natale works in the family bakery by day, but at night her velvet mask and G-string drive men wild. Her double life is a secret, even from Nick Santori, the club's hot new bodyguard who's always treated her like a kid. Now she's planning to show the man of her dreams that while it's okay to look, it's *much* better to touch....

#348 SWEPT AWAY Dawn Atkins
Sex on the Beach

Her plan was simple. Candy Calder would use her vacation to show her boss Matt Rockwell she was serious about her job. But her plan backfired when he invited her to enjoy the sinful side of Malibu. With an offer this tempting, what girl could refuse?

#349 SHIVER AND SPICE Kelley St. John
The Sexth Sense, Bk. 3

She's not alive. She's not dead. She's something in between. And medium Dax Vicknair wants her desperately! Dax fell madly in love with teacher Celeste Beauchamp when he helped one of her students cross over. He thought he was destined to live without her. But now Celeste is back—and Dax intends to make the most of their borrowed time.

#350 THE NAKED TRUTH Shannon Hollis
Million Dollar Secrets, Bk. 3

Risk taker Eve Best is on the verge of having everything she's ever wanted. But what she really wants is the handsome buttoned-down executive Mitchell Hayes, who must convince the gorgeous talk-show host to say "yes" to his business offer *and* his very private proposition....

www.eHarlequin.com

HBCNM0807